Finding Harper had put her in danger. He felt responsible for her. Whether Harper thought so or not.

"I've been found. Your mission is complete, Logan. I don't know why I even agreed to let you stand guard tonight, but you did that, too. Now it's over. The bad guy is gone. I'm safe. Don't put yourself at any more risk on my account."

She sounded tired, and he wondered what it must feel like to go from a peaceful and quiet existence to chaos and trouble.

"My job," he responded, "is filled with risk. This is no different."

"It is, because this isn't your job anymore. You did what you were paid for," she argued.

"We're wasting time discussing it," he said. "Every minute that we spend talking, the guy after you is a little closer to escaping."

"If he's injured, he'll show up at a hospital. The police can arrest him there."

"I'm not taking chances. That's not how I work. I led the guy here. I'm going to make sure he's caught."

Aside from her faith and her family, there's not much **Shirlee McCoy** enjoys more than a good book! When she's not teaching or chauffeuring her five kids, she can usually be found plotting her next Love Inspired Suspense story or wandering around the beautiful Inland Northwest in search of inspiration. Shirlee loves to hear from readers. If you have time, drop her a line at shirlee@shirleemccoy.com.

Books by Shirlee McCoy

Love Inspired Suspense

Visit the Author Profile page at Harlequin.com for more titles.

DEADLY
CHRISTMAS
SECRETS

SHIRLEE MCCOY

HARLEQUIN® LOVE INSPIRED® SUSPENSE

Recycling programs
for this product may
not exist in your area.

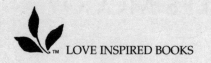 LOVE INSPIRED BOOKS

ISBN-13: 978-0-373-67719-1

Deadly Christmas Secrets

Copyright © 2015 by Shirlee McCoy

www.Harlequin.com

Printed in U.S.A.

Show me Your unfailing love in wonderful ways.
By Your mighty power You rescue those who
seek refuge from their enemies.
—Psalms 17:7

To my parents, Ed and Shirley Porter. Again. Because they are a beautiful example of what forever love means.

– ONE

Tires on gravel.

The sound of a visitor.

An unexpected one, and that made Harper Shelby stop, her back still bent over the shovel, the deep red clay just under its lip.

She didn't get visitors.

Not ever.

And that was the way she liked it. It was the reason she'd bought twenty acres out in the middle of nowhere, and it was the reason she'd stayed there. The cabin had been nothing when she'd moved in—just four walls and a loft, a tiny kitchen meant to be used by hunters. She'd made it into something beautiful—a two-story structure with just enough room for her and her dog. One bedroom upstairs. One bathroom. An office on the lower level. A kitchen that was small but functional. A living area and wood-burning stove that heated the place in the winter.

The kiln at the back of the cleared acre that the cabin sat on.

It had cost a small fortune, but she'd earned a small fortune playing with the clay she pulled from the creek beds on the property. Lydia would have laughed at that if she'd been alive. Harper's older sister had been like that—filled with amusement at life and the people in it. She wouldn't have missed the irony of Harper's new career. No more clean and sterilized office in one of DC's most prestigious graphic design firms. No more climbing the corporate ladder, working to impress a boss, earning a bonus, getting the best clients. No more neat brownstone with all the amenities Harper and Lydia hadn't grown up with. Now Harper shaped clay, molding it into pots and vases and plates that people seemed willing to pay top dollar for. Every one of the pieces was signed with Harper's pseudonym—Ryan A. Harper. Lydia's middle name. Harper's first. *A* for Amelia, Lydia's daughter. Harper would have chosen Ryan Amelia Harper, but she'd been afraid the news voyeurs would recognize the combination of names and come looking for her.

Too many people wanted to hear Lydia and Amelia's story firsthand, and Harper wasn't willing to tell it. Not to reporters or true-crime writers. Not even to the police. Not anymore.

The case was closed, her sister's murderer dead, Amelia presumed dead, too.

Four years was a long time.

Most people had forgotten, but someone hadn't. Someone had sent her a package. It had been shoved into the PO box she kept in a town fifty miles away. It wasn't connected to her new life, her new address or her new property. It was the last vestige of who she'd been, the last connection to her sister's husband, to the friends she'd once had, the busy life she'd once lived. She'd been thinking that it was time to let the box go. It had been empty every time she'd opened it for the better part of two years.

Until this last time.

She'd made the trip the previous day, opened the box and found an envelope shoved inside. She'd opened it with more curiosity than anything. There was no return address. Just a postmark from DC. Inside, she'd found a newspaper clipping—a tiny little section circled. Just a couple of lines about the death of Norman Meyers—a man who'd been convicted of killing Lydia Wilson and her four-year-old daughter, Amelia. There'd been a scrap of fabric, too, a little square of what looked like a pink blanket.

It couldn't have been Amelia's blanket. That had disappeared four years ago, but Harper hadn't been able to shake the sick dread she'd felt looking at those two things. She'd put a call in to the DC homicide detective who'd handled the case. She hadn't heard back from Thomas Willard yet.

She'd planned to give it another day or two and then call again, but the sound of tires on her gravel driveway made her think that Detective Willard might have come to her. Or sent someone to her. A local police officer, maybe?

She left the shovel standing up in the rich, moist earth. This was her favorite creek bed, the colors of the clay rich and vibrant. Soon, though, it would be too cold to dig. Already the ground was hardening. If she didn't harvest what she needed soon, she'd have to wait until spring thaw.

She'd finish collecting today, but first she had to see who was rolling along the road that led to her cabin. She whistled for Picasso but didn't wait for the dog to appear. He loved the woods, loved exploring the thickets and the deer paths. He always returned when she whistled for him, though, and she could hear him bounding along behind her as she headed up the steep path that led to the cabin.

Less than a tenth of a mile, but the incline made going difficult. By the time she reached the edge of the tree line, the sound of tires on gravel had faded. So had the sound of squirrels scurrying around hunting for food. The forest was usually busy this time of year, animals collecting as much food as they could before winter took hold. By mid-December, the landscape went silent and still. Harper did her best work then, snow and ice and heavy gray clouds making her feel as if she was alone in the world.

Until the world intruded.

Once a month, the church ladies came to visit. Last winter, one of the deacons had come to chop wood for her. She hadn't had the heart to tell him that she'd chopped plenty during the summer and fall, so she'd let him do it and then tried to pay him for his efforts. He'd refused to take money, so she'd given him a vase crafted from clay she'd harvested, fired to perfection and then glazed with all the colors of winter.

Picasso halted at the edge of the trees, growling low in his throat, his scruff standing on end. She stopped beside him, touching his head.

"What do you see, Picasso?" she murmured, peering out from between thick pine boughs.

She'd been expecting a police cruiser.

A black Jeep was there instead.

She couldn't see the driver, but no one she knew drove a Jeep. She took a step back, her fingers sliding through Picasso's collar. He might be growling, but if someone got out of the car and offered a treat, he'd be all over that in a heartbeat.

She didn't want the Irish wolfhound anywhere near whoever was driving the Jeep because she had a bad feeling about her visitor, a feeling that said she'd be better off staying in the woods than stepping out where the driver could see her.

The driver's door opened, and a man climbed out. Tall. Very tall. Very muscular. Blond hair. Eyes shielded by sunglasses. He wore dark jeans, a black T-shirt and a jacket with a patch in the shape of a heart stitched to the right shoulder.

A uniform of some sort?

She wasn't going to ask.

She wasn't going to step out from the trees, either. Her property was too far off the beaten path for someone to find his way there accidentally. This guy had come for a purpose. She'd rather have someone else around when she found out what that was. She couldn't call one of the church ladies, and she didn't have any close guy friends. She'd call the sheriff's department. They could send deputies out, and she'd just stay in the woods until they arrived.

She pulled her phone from her coat pocket, watching as the guy took a step away from the Jeep. Picasso barked twice, the happy greeting ringing through the still morning air. The man turned in their direction, scanning the tree line.

She didn't think he could see her through the thick pine boughs, but she took a step back anyway, pulling Picasso with her.

"You can come out," the man called, taking off his sunglasses as if that would somehow make him look less menacing. "I don't bite."

"My dog does," she responded, and he shrugged.

"I've had worse than a dog bite. My name is Logan Fitzgerald. Your brother-in-law sent me."

"My brother-in-law has no idea I'm here," she responded, keeping the pine boughs between them. Despite what she'd said, she would have been very surprised if Picasso took a bite out of anyone. He was a friendly dog, easygoing and funny. He served as a good early-warning system if a bear or mountain lion was around, and she liked to think he'd try to protect her if one came along, but he had yet to have to prove himself.

"Maybe I should rephrase that," Logan said. "Gabe Wilson hired the company I work for to find you."

"Why?"

"He had some information he wanted to share with you."

"I'm not interested."

He cocked his head to the side, and despite the foliage between them, she was sure he was taking in her mud-splattered jeans, her hiking boots, the thick wool coat she wore over her T-shirt. "All right. I'll give him the message for you."

"That's it?"

"He hired us to find you, Harper." He drawled her name, just a bit of a Southern accent in the words. "When he did, he signed a contract stating that if you don't want to be found, you simply have to say so. He gets no address. No phone number. Nothing."

"That doesn't seem like something Gabe would agree to." Her brother-in-law never gave up on anything. He was determined and driven to a fault. At least, he had been four years ago.

"He didn't have a choice. That's the way HEART works."

"HEART?"

"We're a freelance security and hostage rescue team," he responded as if that explained everything. "I'll pass along your message." He slid into the Jeep and would have closed the door, but the sound of an engine drifted from somewhere down the road. He frowned. "You expecting company?"

"No."

"I guess I'll stick around, see who's coming."

"That's not necessary."

"Sure it is." He crossed the distance between them and pulled back the pine bough that hung closest to her face. "But it really isn't necessary for you to keep hiding from me. If I'd wanted to hurt you, I'd have done it by now."

"That's…comforting."

"You know what would be comforting, Harper? The idea that someone who lives out in the middle of nowhere and tromps through the woods every day looking for mud—"

"Clay," she corrected him, and he nodded.

"*Clay*. What would make me feel comfortable is the idea that this person was carrying a firearm."

"I have bear spray."

"Bear spray isn't going to take down a guy who's a dozen feet away, pointing a gun at you."

"I—"

"Guy's coming fast," he said, cutting her off and moving into the tree line.

"How can you t—?"

Before she could finish the question, a black sedan was racing into view. Picasso barked excitedly. Two visitors was a dream come true. He lunged toward the driveway, breaking from Harper's hold.

She followed without thinking, lunging out into the open, the car barreling down on them.

She had about three seconds to realize it wasn't going to stop, three seconds to think about the fact that whoever was driving had every intention of mowing her down.

And then she was tackled from behind, rolled toward the trees again.

Tires squealed. Someone shouted.

Logan?

And then the world exploded, dirt flying up from the ground near her head, dead leaves jumping into the air, dust and debris and the acrid scent of gunfire stinging her nose.

Logan Fitzgerald had a split second to realize he'd been used before the first bullet flew. He didn't like it. Didn't like that he'd been used to find a woman whom someone apparently wanted dead.

Gabe Wilson?

Probably, but Logan didn't have time to think about it. Not now. Later he'd figure things out.

For now, he just had to stay alive, keep Harper alive.

He pulled his handgun, fired a shot into the front windshield of the dark sedan. Not a kill shot, but it was enough to take out the glass, cause a distraction.

He rolled off Harper's prone form and shoved

her toward the tree line. "Go!" he shouted, firing another shot, this one in the front tire.

She scrambled into the bushes, her giant dog following along behind her.

The sedan backed up, tires squealing as the driver tried to speed away. Not an easy task with a flat tire, and Logan caught a glimpse of two men. One dark haired. One bald. He fired toward the gunman and saw the bald guy duck as the bullet slammed into what remained of the windshield.

He could have pursued them, shot out another tire, tried to take them both down. This was what he was trained to do—face down the opponent, win. But Harper had run into the woods. He didn't know how far, didn't know if she was out of range of the gunman or close enough to take a stray bullet.

He knew what he wanted to do—pursue the gunman, find out who had hired him, find out why.

He also knew what his boss, Chance Miller, would say—protect the innocent first. Worry about the criminals later.

He'd have been right.

Logan knew it, but he still wanted to hunt the gunmen down.

He holstered his gun and stepped into the

trees, the sound of the car thumping along the gravel road ringing through the early morning.

Sunlight streamed in through the tree canopy, glinting off leaves still wet from the previous night's rain. He'd stayed in a tiny bed-and-breakfast at the edge of a national park, waiting for sunrise to come. He hadn't wanted to drive out to Harper's place in the middle of the night. If he'd known he had a tail, he wouldn't have driven out at all.

He scowled, moving down a steep embankment, following a trail of footprints in the damp earth. He could hear a creek babbling, the quiet melody belying the violence that had just occurred.

The car engine died, the thump of tires ceasing.

A door opened. Closed.

Was the gunman pursuing them?

He lost the trail of footprints at a creek that tripped along the base of a deep embankment. A bucket was there, sitting near the water, half filled with red mud.

Clay, Harper had said.

He didn't think it would matter much if they were both dead.

He wanted to call to her, draw her out of her hiding place, but the forest had gone dead silent. Years of working in some of the most dangerous places in Afghanistan had honed his senses. Even now, years after he'd left the military to raise his younger siblings, he knew when trouble was lurking nearby.

He moved cautiously, keeping low as he crossed the creek and searched for footprints in the mucky earth. The scent of dead leaves filled his nose, the late November air slicing through his jacket. He ignored the cold. Ignored everything but his mission—finding Harper Shelby and keeping her alive.

He moved up the embankment, dropping to the ground as leaves crackled behind him. Whoever was coming wasn't being quiet about it. Not Harper. She'd moved like a wraith, disappearing into the forest with barely a sound.

He eased behind a thick oak, adrenaline pumping through him as he waited for his quarry. It didn't take long. A few more loud snaps of branches and crackles of leaves and the bald man appeared, inching his way down toward the creek, his belly hanging over a belt that was cinched so tight, Logan was surprised the guy could breathe.

He could have taken him out then, fired one shot that would bring the guy down for good, but he was more interested in hearing what he had to say and knowing why he was trying to kill Harper.

He waited, counting footsteps as the guy drew closer.

Another few yards and he'd be within reach. Another few feet. The guy moved past the tree where Logan was hiding, completely oblivious to the danger he was in. Not a professional hired gun, that was for sure. Logan had run into his fair share of those during the years he'd been working for HEART. They weren't this careless, and they were never easy to take down.

He waited another heartbeat.

That was all it took. Just that second of waiting, and calm became chaos. The bushes beside the guy moved and Harper's dog burst out, snarling and barking as he tried to bite the bald guy.

The man cursed, raising his weapon, aiming at the dog's head, and then Harper was there, a shovel in hand. She swung hard, the metal end of the tool smacking into the guy's wrist as Logan pulled his weapon and fired.

TWO

The bald guy looked dead. His eyes were closed and blood was seeping from a wound in his shoulder. He was breathing, though, his barrel chest rising and falling.

Harper dropped the shovel and leaned over him. She would have touched the pulse point in his neck, but Logan edged in beside her and nudged her away.

He lifted the man's gun from the ground, unloaded it, then shoved the cartridge in his pocket.

"He needs first aid," she murmured, trying to move closer again.

He blocked her way, frisking the guy, pulling a knife from the sheath strapped to his calf.

"First things first, Harper," Logan muttered. "We secure the weapons. Then we provide first aid. It's in the rule book."

"What rule book is that?" she asked, shrugging out of her jacket and using it to staunch the blood flowing from the bald guy's shoulder.

He moaned. Not dead after all.

"The one called *How to Keep Alive in Dangerous Situations*," Logan responded drily. "Did you call the police?"

"Yes." As soon as she'd cleared the tree line, she'd called 911. The dispatcher had assured her help was on the way.

Good thing she hadn't had to depend on that. She'd be dead now.

She pressed harder on the bleeding wound. The guy had been shooting at her, but that didn't mean she wanted him dead.

"Get off me!" he growled, rolling onto his side and struggling to his feet. His wrist was broken from the force of her blow, his face ashen, but he looked more angry than anything.

"How about you mind your manners, buddy?" Logan said calmly, holstering his weapon.

"How about you shut up?" the guy spit out, his voice a little slurred, his gaze darting back the way they'd come. No one was there, but Harper thought he must be hoping for help.

"Fine by me." Logan pulled a cell phone from his pocket, typed something into it and snapped a picture of the man.

"Hey! What's that about?" the guy snarled.

"Just sending your mug shot to a friend who

can find out who you are and whether or not you have any warrants out for your arrest."

"You got nothing on me."

"You tried to shoot us," Harper responded, and the guy grinned.

"Thought you were deer. Hard to see people out in woods like this."

"No one is going to believe that," she said, and Logan touched her shoulder, his fingers warm through her T-shirt.

"Don't engage him, Harper. He's got his story. It's what he'll tell the police. He'll still end up in jail."

"Not if I have anything to do with it," the guy responded, his gaze darting toward the creek.

"You think your friend is coming for you?" Logan asked, brushing dirt from his jeans, his expression unreadable. He had dark eyes. Not brown. Not black. Midnight blue. They remained fixed on the gunman, no hint of emotion in them. "Because he's not."

"We're a team—"

"A team that kills for money?" Logan smiled, a hard, predatory curve of the lips that would have made Harper's blood run cold if she'd been on the receiving end of it. "That's the kind of team that lasts until one guy gets caught. Then it's not a team. It's just that one guy alone, wishing he'd picked some other way to make money."

"You don't know—"

An engine roared to life and tires thumped on gravel. First slowly, then more quickly.

The man's accomplice escaping while he had the chance? Probably, and the man seemed to know it. He pivoted and tried to run into the trees.

Logan moved so quickly, Harper barely had time to realize what he was doing. One minute he was beside her. The next he and the bald guy were on the ground, Logan's knee pressed into the other man's back.

"Not smart, buddy," Logan said quietly. "Stuff like that could get a man killed."

"I'm not your buddy, and I'm not the one who's going to die." The guy bucked, trying to dislodge Logan. He didn't have a chance. Even if he hadn't been weak from blood loss, Harper didn't think he could have moved Logan. Muscles and training definitely trumped anger.

"I guess that depends on whether or not you try to run when the cops get here."

"When the cops get here—"

"Tell you what," Logan interrupted. "How about we skip the discussion and get to the point. Who hired you to follow me out here?"

The guy went silent, his face blazing with anger.

"Right. So someone did hire you."

"I didn't say that!" the man snarled.

"Which answers another question. You're afraid of whoever hired you, and that's why you're denying it."

"I'm not—"

Sirens cut off the words, the screaming sound of them filling the woods. Picasso barked frantically, excited and alarmed by the chaos.

Harper just wanted it to be over.

She wanted the police to take the gunman away. She wanted Logan to leave. She wanted to go back to the life she'd made for herself. Quiet. Simple. Free of disappointments and heartaches and sorrows.

She supposed that made her a coward.

She wasn't really.

She'd loved the life she'd once had—the hectic, high-stress graphic design job, the sweet brownstone she'd bought for a steal and remodeled. She'd loved her sister, her niece. She'd even fallen in love. Once upon a time. When she'd still been in college and not nearly as convinced that Shelby women always chose men who were going to hurt them.

Daniel had taught her a valuable lesson about that.

If she hadn't learned it from her college sweetheart, she might have learned it from watching Lydia. Gabe hadn't been the kind of husband any woman deserved. He'd cheated. More than once, and he hadn't been apologetic about it.

And then Lydia and Amelia had died, murdered by a homeless man who'd stolen Lydia's purse. That was the story the prosecuting attorney told. He'd built a tight case and presented it to a jury, convincing them that Norman Meyers had killed Lydia and Amelia and tossed their bodies into the Patuxent River. Norman was a known meth addict who'd committed enough petty crimes to be a frequent flyer with the police. He'd been married twice, and both his wives had restraining orders against him. *Violent* was a word that had been used a lot during the trial, and Norman's angry, defiant glare hadn't done anything to convince the jury otherwise. Despite the fact that Amelia's body had never been found, the prosecuting attorney had gone for two counts of second-degree murder. He'd gotten what he'd wanted, and Norman had been put away for life.

Harper had always thought she should be happy with that, but she'd felt no sense of closure. Most days she could convince herself that the jury was right, that Norman was guilty. There were other days when she thought it was all a little too convenient—Lydia and Amelia sneaking out of her place in the middle of the night, walking along a street quiet enough for them to be accosted without any witnesses. Amelia's body missing and never found. Harper's brother-in-law finally free of a wife he'd seemed to despise. Harper had spent enough time with her sister and brother-in-law to hear the arguments, the accusations, the veiled threats. She knew that Gabe loved his daughter. He would have never been able to hurt her, but Harper wasn't sure that he wouldn't have hurt Lydia.

Had he killed her? Secreted their daughter away somewhere?

The idea seemed farfetched. Besides, the only family member the police seemed to have suspected was Harper. She'd been the last person to see her niece and sister alive and—according to her brother-in-law—was a jealous younger sister who'd hated Lydia.

The press had had a field day with stories that implicated her. She'd lost a few clients because of it, and then she'd lost her job.

Worse, she'd had no alibi, no way of proving that her sister and niece had left her house alive. Until Norman Meyers had pawned Lydia's engagement ring, Harper had been certain she was going to be tried and convicted.

Not good memories. Any of them.

She shuddered, taking a step away from Logan and the man he was still holding down.

"Harper?" Logan said sharply, and she

thought he must have already tried to get her attention. "Can you head to your place and lead the police here?"

"Why?" the gunman spat. "Because you plan to murder me and don't want any witnesses?"

Logan ignored him, pulling out his cell phone and glancing at the screen. "Tell the police that I've got Langley Simmons here. Looks as if he has a warrant out for his arrest."

The gunman cursed, tried to twist out from under Logan.

"Harper?" Logan prodded.

"I'll get them," she responded, calling to Picasso and jogging away. She wanted to leave both men behind, leave the entire mess behind.

She knew she couldn't, of course.

She'd spent her life trying to do the right thing, trying to live the way she'd thought she should—following the rules, being moral and just and kind. She'd wanted what her mother had never been able to achieve—stability, security, edifying relationships.

God had obviously had other plans.

Her life had taken a turn she hadn't anticipated, and now all she wanted was to be at peace.

It didn't look as if that was going to happen, either.

But God was in control.

He had a plan and a way.

She just wished He'd tell her what it was.

There was a lesson in trust there, she supposed, but she'd never been good at trusting. Even when it came to God. Maybe especially then. She'd prayed a lot when she was a kid, begging God to step in before the family was evicted or the lights were turned off or the police came to search for the drugs one of her mother's boyfriends had left.

Most of the time, those prayers hadn't been answered. At least not in any way that made sense to her. Lights were often turned off and evictions happened. As an adult, she knew those were natural consequences to her mother's habitual sins, but those old feelings of distrust and anxiety were still there.

She pushed aside the memories as she raced up the steep hill that led to her cabin. Picasso bounded out of the woods in front of her, and she heard a masculine voice call his name. Sheriff Jeb Hunter or one of his deputies.

Seconds later, she hit the top of the path and ran out onto her driveway. Two police cars were parked close to the cabin, Jeb Hunter crouched next to one of them shooting pictures of a bullet casing. Picasso lay a few feet away, panting quietly.

Jeb looked up as Harper approached, his deep

green eyes shaded by a uniform hat. "Heard there was trouble out here, Harper. From the look of things, that might be true."

"It is."

"Want to tell me what happened?"

"Someone was shooting at us."

"Us?"

"A guy my brother-in-law sent. He showed up a few minutes before the guys with the guns."

"There's more than one gunman?"

"Yes. One drove away. One of them is in the woods, injured."

"The guy your brother-in-law sent? Where's he?"

"Keeping the injured guy from running."

"Then, I guess we'd better go find them. Want to lead the way?"

Not really. What she wanted to do was go back to her clay. It wasn't a possibility, so she whistled for Picasso and headed back into the woods.

Logan didn't much like stepping aside and letting other people handle problems. Right now, he didn't have a choice. He wasn't a cop and hadn't been hired to work with them, so he hung back, watching as Simmons was loaded onto a stretcher, his wrist handcuffed to a deputy sheriff.

Sheriff Jeb Hunter wasn't taking any chances. That was good. Simmons was desperate. Given the opportunity, he'd run. If he did that, Logan doubted he'd ever be found. If he was, it would probably just be his body that turned up. The guy was scared of someone. Logan wanted to know who, but all Simmons was willing to admit to was a few too many beers and a case of mistaken identity.

Lies, but it didn't matter.

The guy was guilty of nearly killing someone, and he'd be in jail for a while. Maybe when his buddy didn't show up to bail him out, he'd be more willing to talk.

"So, Logan Fitzgerald," Sheriff Hunter said as the ambulance pulled away. "You want to explain how you happened to be in the right place at the right time?"

"I was hired by Gabe Wilson."

"My brother-in-law," Harper interrupted as if those words would explain everything.

They explained nothing. Not to the sheriff and not to Logan. Finding Harper had been easy. She'd taken out a loan for property in Westminster, Maryland. No address was listed, but with only a little digging he'd found a house title with her name on it.

Easy.

So why hadn't Gabe done it himself?

The guy had money. Plenty of it.

He could have hired anyone to find his sister-in-law. He'd hired HEART.

Had he known there was going to be trouble?

Or had he simply wanted to hedge his bets, make sure that Harper was found because...

Why?

It had been four years since Harper disappeared from Gabe's life. If he'd wanted to kill her, wouldn't he have made an attempt before?

Lots of questions.

Not many answers.

The sheriff must have felt the same way. He frowned, took off his uniform hat and ran his hand over his dark hair. "Now, why, I'm wondering, would your brother-in-law want to find you?"

Logan responded, "He said he received information about his daughter."

"Amelia is dead," Harper said, her face pale as paper.

"There was a funeral," Logan corrected her, because he'd studied the case, read every article. That was the way he was. He liked to be prepared, to understand all the details before he began a mission. "Her body was never found."

"I know," she said quietly. "What information does he have?"

"A photograph. A piece of cloth that he says might be part of her blanket."

He didn't think it was possible, but she paled more, swaying slightly. Her dog nudged her side.

She touched his head and seemed to ground herself.

"I received something similar."

"A photo?" Sheriff Hunter asked.

"No. A newspaper article and a piece of something that might have been Amelia's favorite blanket." The words rasped out, and Logan cupped her elbow, afraid she might pass out. She looked that shaken, that anxious.

"Did you keep it?" the sheriff asked, and she nodded.

"I called the DC police about it, but they haven't gotten back to me."

"When was that?" Logan asked, leading her toward the two-story cabin that sat in the middle of a cleared lot. An acre. Maybe a little more. He'd looked at the plans before he'd driven out, gotten a good feel for the land. Not because he'd expected trouble. Just because it was what he did.

It had paid off this time.

He knew the topography. The creeks. The flatland and forests. The twenty acres she owned wasn't a lot, but it was enough to get lost in when the forests were as deep and untouched as the ones that surrounded Harper's place.

"Last night. I called Thomas Willard. He's a homicide detective who led the investigation into my sister's murder." She opened the door.

No key.

She obviously hadn't locked up before she'd left.

That bothered him.

Life was filled with danger. A person couldn't avoid it, but he could certainly prepare for it.

"You might want to lock that the next time you go out," he said, and she shrugged, soft brown hair slipping from its clip and falling across her face. She had freckles on her nose and on her cheeks, long black lashes tipped with gold. He'd say that she spent a lot of time outside, and that she knew her land about as well as anyone could know anything. He'd also say that she probably thought she had things under control, that it was within her power to keep trouble from coming down on her head.

That was a dangerous thing to assume.

He wanted to tell her that, but they were strangers, and he was making assumptions based on what he saw—the tidy little two-story cabin, the rifle that looked as if it had never been used hanging above a small fireplace, the wood-burning stove with its neat pile of wood beside it. Unless he missed his guess, there was more piled by the back door, several cords of it in storage on a back porch or in a shed. She probably had a month's worth of supplies, an emergency generator for lights, everything she thought she'd ever need. That was good. Great, even. But the best-laid plans didn't always pan out.

"It's never been a concern before," she said, tucking the stray hair behind her ear, her fingers speckled with flecks of red mud. "Now that it is, I'll be sure to lock up. If you gentlemen don't mind waiting here, the package is upstairs. I'll get it."

She ran from the room, heading toward the back of the cabin, her dog following along behind her. Logan figured there was a kitchen there, maybe a small laundry room and the staircase that led up to the second story. He was curious to see the place, get a feel for how difficult it would be to secure.

He stayed where he was, though, because he'd been asked to, and because he had a few things he wanted to talk to the sheriff about.

"Have your men found the sedan?" he asked as footsteps tapped across the floor above his head.

"Not yet, but the guy can't have gotten far. Not with a blown tire."

"There are plenty of places to hide around here," Logan pointed out. "I'd guess he pulled onto some side road, hid the car and took off on foot."

"I'm guessing you're right, and since there are only a few crossroads between Harper's property and town, I'm feeling pretty confident we'll track the car down quickly."

"And then?"

"Take some dogs into the woods, see if we can find our guy."

"In the meantime, Harper will be out here alone."

"You think the guy is going to come back?" Sheriff Hunter asked.

"I think he didn't accomplish his goal. Harper is still alive."

"You're assuming Harper was the target," Sheriff Hunter pointed out.

"That seems like a logical assumption."

"In my opinion, it would be just as logical to assume that someone is after you. In your line of work, that wouldn't be unlikely." Logan didn't ask how he knew what kind of work Logan did. If Sheriff Hunter hadn't heard about the visitor to his small town the previous night and checked things out, he'd have had people checking Logan's credentials as soon as he'd gotten the plate number off the Jeep.

"It wouldn't be, but there were a dozen opportunities to take me out on my drive here. Not to mention my sleepover in Dora's Sleep Haven last night. Place has no security. The windows don't even lock."

Sheriff Hunter smirked. "You should have asked a local. We would have pointed you to our pastor. He has a nice in-law suite that he loans out to anyone who has a need."

"In other words, I'm the first person ever to stay with Dora?"

"There was a guy a few years back. Turned out he was running from the law and wanted a place to hide out. Not so smart to hide in a town that has fewer than a thousand residents. Dora called me. I did a little checking. Guy ended up spending the next night in Snowy Vista's town jail."

"Probably a lot more comfortable than Dora's place," Logan muttered.

"Probably." He walked to the fireplace and lifted the shotgun. "Not loaded. I'm not keen on her living out here on her own, but if she's going to stay, it would be a good idea to have some security."

"You planning to talk to her about it?" he asked. If Sheriff Hunter didn't, Logan would. She needed protection. At least until the guy who'd been driving the sedan was caught.

"I'll give it a try. She has her own way of doing things. Not sure she's going to listen to me."

"She will if she wants to stay alive," Logan responded as Harper walked back into the room.

THREE

Amelia.

She was all Harper could think about as she paced her bedroom, the sound of voices drifting up through the floorboards. Logan's voice. The higher-pitched voice of his coworker, Stella Silverstone. She'd arrived three hours ago, striding into the cabin as if she owned the place. She'd made tea, fed Picasso, acted as if it wasn't any of her concern if Harper didn't want twenty-four-hour protection at the cabin.

"It's her business," Stella had said when Logan and Sheriff Hunter insisted that Harper shouldn't stay in the cabin alone. "If she wants to die before she finds out if her niece is alive, what's it to you?"

That was it.

All it took.

That one thought, that one little hope that Amelia was alive was enough to make Harper put up with anything or anyone.

Amelia alive…

Her pulse raced at the thought, her throat tight with dozens of memories—her niece's birth, all the little and big moments that had happened after it.

There'd been times during the past few years when she'd wondered if Amelia was out there somewhere, waiting to be found. Now the possibility seemed real. That little piece of blanket, the newspaper article—had they been hints? Clues designed to pull Harper closer to the truth, closer to her niece?

Or bring her closer to her death?

She shuddered.

She'd kept to herself for years, had separated herself from her old life. She'd put the past behind her, and now it was in front of her again.

Why now?

For what purpose?

She needed to talk to Gabe. She'd called him, left a message on his machine. He hadn't returned her call. He'd probably make her wait a few days. That was the way he was. The way he'd always been. Everything in his time frame. He and Lydia had been late or early to social events on his whim. They hadn't even made it to Harper's college graduation because Gabe had decided that they needed to go over the household budget.

A joke, because Lydia had no control over their finances. She hadn't even been told how much her husband made. She'd known about the heirloom jewelry he kept in his wall safe, though, and she'd figured out the combination. When Lydia had wanted something, she'd figured out how to get it. She hadn't really wanted to attend Harper's graduation. She hadn't wanted to leave her cheating husband because that would mean giving up the fancy house, the nice clothes, the cash allowance.

Whatever anyone said, whatever anyone believed, Harper had always thought that had cost Lydia her life.

Harper shut the thought off, pulling back the curtains and looking out into the growing darkness. Night fell early this time of year, but there were still a few golden rays of sun glinting on the horizon. In the distance, she could see Snowy Vista, the lights from the town gleaming through the trees. Soon the place would be decorated for Christmas. Every door would have a wreath, every window colorful lights. Trees would be decked out with garland, and yards would boast Nativity scenes and snowmen. She didn't have anyone to shop for, but every year, she went to town the week before Christmas. Every year, she walked Main Street, looked at all the Christmas decorations, listened to the carols drifting from shops and watched the people walking up and down the street. It was a small town, but near the holidays, people came in from Baltimore and DC, or traveled down from Lancaster and York, just to see the Christmas displays.

That was the kind of town Snowy Vista was. Not a place most people stayed. Not even for a night. Just a place to pass through, to admire in the way one would look at a bouquet of flowers or a snowy mountain peak.

"It's pretty, though. If I wanted to live around people again, it wouldn't be a bad place to settle," she said, and Picasso huffed his agreement, his cold nose touching her hand.

A light flashed in the trees and she frowned, leaning closer to the glass, trying to see if someone was out there. Sheriff Hunter's men hadn't found the sedan or its driver yet. The guy would be a fool to return, but that didn't mean he wouldn't.

Another flash, and she stepped away from the window, watching as the light flashed again. A signal of some sort? Should she tell Logan? She headed toward the door and was nearly there when it flew open.

Stella strode in. "Let's go."

"Where?"

"Away from here," she responded, grabbing Harper's hand and dragging her out of the room.

"For how long? Because if we're going to be gone for more than a few hours—"

"Less talking, more moving," Stella interjected, her short red hair bouncing as she hurried Harper down the stairs and into the kitchen. It was dark there. No light spilling in from the living room or from the office that jutted off the back of the house.

"What's going on?" she whispered, afraid to speak too loudly, afraid that if she did, whatever was causing them to rush from the cabin would find them.

"Someone's out in the woods making a nice little circle of the property. Logan thinks it's best if we clear out for a while."

"And go where?"

"Does it matter?" Stella opened the front door, pulled her to a cherry-red SUV and opened the car door. "Get in."

"Picasso!" she called as she climbed in.

The dog skidded outside and bounded toward the SUV, and then he stopped. Dead still. Every muscle in his body taut, he eyed the dark woods at the edge of the property, growled and then raced toward the tree line.

"Picasso," she called again, but Stella had

already slammed the door and jumped into the driver's seat.

"I can't leave my dog," she said, reaching for the door handle.

"Logan will get him."

"Logan doesn't know he's missing!" she protested, but they were already racing along the gravel road. There were no streetlights out this far. No moonlight glimmering from the steely sky. Stella didn't turn on her headlights, and the road was shadowy, the trees looming up on either side. Anything could be lurking out there, anyone.

A light flashed, and the SUV shuddered, swerving toward the trees, then back toward the road again. Harper could feel the thump of a flat tire. Someone was firing at them, and one tire had already been shot out.

Stella didn't slow down, just kept speeding through the darkness.

"Get down!" she shouted, jerking the wheel to the left. Seconds later, the back window exploded, shards of glass flying through the air, falling on Harper's hair, her hands, her arms. She could see them shimmering in the dashboard lights. She could feel the awful thud of her heart, the rapid pulse of the blood through her veins.

She'd been scared earlier. Terrified, even,

but she'd thought the danger was over. She had wanted to believe that the man who'd been driving the sedan had disappeared—gone for good.

She'd been wrong.

If she hadn't allowed Logan and Stella to stay...

What?

Would Picasso have warned her in time? Would Harper have been able to load the shotgun? Protect herself from the threat?

"Something is burning," Stella said so calmly, the words didn't register with Harper.

The smell did—the sharp scent of gasoline, the acrid smell of smoke.

"Must have hit the gas line and sparked. We need to get out, but we need to be smart about it," Stella continued as if she were talking about the color of the sky or the temperature of the air.

"Smart? Smart would be getting out while we have the chance," Harper exclaimed, grabbing her door handle.

"Smart would be staying alive. The likelihood this car is going to explode is little to none. The likelihood one of us is going to be shot dead by the guy who's after you? That's higher. You get out your side, and you'll be in the middle of the road. We're getting out on my side. Back door, because it's right up against the trees. You go over the seat first. I'll follow."

Harper scrambled over the seat, the scents of gasoline and smoke getting stronger. She didn't see flames, but she was sure the interior of the SUV was growing hotter.

She reached the door and jerked at the handle. She scrambled for the lock, her fingers shaking as she tried to find it.

"Calm down," Stella barked so close to her ear, she jumped. "Panicking gets people nowhere really fast."

She reached past Harper and unlocked the vehicle.

"Let's go," she urged, pressing close as Harper stepped into the scratchy embrace of a spruce. The scent of evergreen needles mixed with gasoline and smoke, and she gagged, pushing deeper into the trees, the blackness nearly complete there.

She knew the woods like the back of her hand, knew every inch of her property, but they'd gone beyond that, traveling a few miles down the gravel road. She thought she was heading toward the creek. Branches scratched at her face, pulled at her hair and ripped at her clothes, but she kept a steady pace, heading deeper into the woods, and hopefully farther away from the danger.

She thought she heard the creek up ahead and was heading for that when something crashed through the brush beside her, the sound bringing to life every nightmare she'd ever had, every secret fear.

Stella said something, but she didn't hear. She was too busy running, sprinting through the woods as if it was an open field, everything inside telling her to go and keep going.

She slammed into something.

Not a tree. A man. His chest hard, his body tall and firm.

She tried to jump back, but strong arms wrapped around her, pulling her in. She struggled against the hold, tore at the arms, used every fighting tactic she'd learned as a kid growing up in one of the roughest neighborhoods in DC, because she wasn't going to die in the woods. Not before she found out the truth about Amelia.

"Calm down," Logan said, grabbing Harper's fist just before it connected with his jaw. "It's me."

"Logan?" She stilled, her arms dropping to her sides, her eyes wide in the darkness.

She'd come barreling out of the woods as if a couple of bears were chasing after her, but he couldn't hear anything but the quiet burble of the creek and the soft rasp of her breath.

"You nearly scared the life out me," she said, stepping away from him, her voice a little shaky.

"Where's Stella?" he asked, because there was no way his coworker had left Harper to fend for herself. Not if she were capable of anything else.

"Right here," Stella responded, stepping through the thick trees to his right. "With the dog. If the perp is still around, I haven't seen him. Not since he destroyed my brand-new car."

"I took a shot at him after he hit your fuel line. I was a little out of range, but I think I might have hit him."

"That explains why he didn't wait around for us to get out of the SUV," Stella responded drily.

"He's heading east. Straight toward the highway."

"That's five miles away," Harper commented, her hand on Picasso's head. She looked smaller in the darkness, her body diminished by the vast forest surrounding them.

"Five miles isn't all that far," Stella responded. "Not for someone who's desperate, and he is. He sticks around here and the police are going to catch him. Or one of us will."

"One of us is planning to," Logan said, pulling a Maglite from his coat pocket. He hadn't used it before, but now that the perp was on the run, he'd take every advantage he could to hunt the guy down before he made it to the highway.

"Are you going to try to track him?" Stella asked. She'd let him take the lead on this. That was the way Stella was. No fuss. No muss. If it wasn't her assignment, she took a backseat, followed orders, made herself as much of an asset to the team as she could.

"He's heading for his escape vehicle. I want to get to him before he reaches it."

"The police could do the job as easily," she remarked. No judgment in the words. Just a statement of fact. "And you know how Chance is—he likes to let the local PD handle their problems."

"This isn't their problem. This is my problem. I was hired to—"

"Find Harper. Which you've done."

True, but finding Harper had put her in danger. He felt responsible for that, which made him responsible for her. Whether Chance thought so or not. And whether Harper did or not.

And he didn't think she did.

She hadn't wanted twenty-four-hour protection, had seemed determined to go on the way she had before he'd showed up with a gunman on his tail. She'd finally conceded when Stella had mentioned her niece.

Amelia seemed to be the key to all of this,

and she seemed to be the key to getting Harper to accept protection and help.

"I'm right here," Harper muttered. "I've been found." She sounded tired, and he wondered what it must feel like to go from a peaceful and quiet existence to chaos and trouble.

"And now you're in danger."

"Not because of you," she responded. "So let's all go back to my place and wait for the police. They can do what they need to, and we can decide the best way to proceed."

That wasn't going to happen.

He wanted this guy, and if he waited for the police to show up, he wasn't going to get him.

He glanced at Stella. "I'll meet you back at the cabin. Can you call the sheriff? Ask him to have someone on the road, searching for the perp? He might want to notify the local hospital, too."

"But—"

"No sense arguing," Stella said, cutting off Harper's protest. "He's stubborn as a mule." She grabbed Harper's arm and dragged her back the way they'd come.

Picasso followed, silent for once. The dog probably sensed the tension in the air, the danger that seemed to lurk just out of sight.

Logan flashed his light on the ground, studying the leaves and foliage for signs that someone had passed that way. Minutes went by, the forest coming to life—small animals scurrying through underbrush, an owl calling from a nearby tree. Thick flakes of snow tumbled through the tree canopy, dancing in the beam of his light. If he didn't hurry, the trail would be lost, the guy gone.

In the distance, sirens were screaming, the police racing in. Hopefully with their K-9 team. The dogs had come up empty earlier, but the scent would be easier to find this time, the area they'd be searching a lot smaller.

His light bounced across the ground, glowing on dead leaves, moist earth and a slick wet splotch halfway hidden by pine needles.

He moved closer and studied the spot.

Blood for sure. A drop that was just beginning to dry. The guy wasn't that far ahead. Maybe the injury was slowing him down, keeping him from escaping to the road.

Or maybe he wasn't running.

Maybe he was waiting in the underbrush, hoping for another chance to strike.

FOUR

Forty-five minutes. A long time to walk through swirling snow and gusting wind. Logan had done worse—hiking desolate regions of Afghanistan in the middle of the night, scaling rock faces and climbing mountains in search of enemy strongholds. He'd been a scout sniper, trained in night operations. He'd probably still be that if his parents hadn't died. He'd loved the work, the adrenaline rush, the high-stakes play.

He'd traded it all for a two-thousand-acre soy farm in North Carolina, which three generations of his family had owned and operated. He hadn't done it because he'd wanted to farm. He'd done it because his father was dead, his mother was missing and his brothers needed him. Five years in the military hadn't prepared him for finishing up the job of raising three teenage boys. They'd had a couple of rocky years, but he'd managed to get them through college and into life without much of a problem. Colton ran the farm now and had turned it into an organic venture that was making way more money than their father had probably ever thought was possible. Trent was the town sheriff. Gavin was pastor of the church they'd attended when they were kids. They were all productive citizens doing what they thought God was calling them to. Their parents would have been proud. Logan was proud. And he was going back for Christmas.

His brothers had begged him. When that hadn't worked, they'd had Andrea call. Colton's wife had a way of convincing anyone of anything, and when she'd mentioned how long it had been since Logan's nieces had seen him, he'd agreed to spend his ten-day Christmas vacation in Rushers, North Carolina.

Those plans weren't going to work out if he died, so he ignored the snow and the wind, the cold that seemed to burrow deep into his bones. He focused on the trail, on the stillness of the forest around him, the dogs coming up behind him.

The perp had to know the police were on his trail, and he had to be panicked. Panicked people made dangerous decisions. Anything was possible. The guy could be just up ahead, waiting to ambush his pursuers. He could be running for the highway. He could be hunkering down, hoping that the snow would wash his scent away.

Logan was prepared for any of those things as he crested a hill and caught sight of the highway—just lights flashing through trees. He moved toward them, the dense foliage thinning as he drew closer to the interstate. The trees were sparser here, snow layering the ground, providing a thick cushion to Logan's footsteps. He searched the ground and found what looked like footprints pressed into fresh snow. The perp had veered off course, heading south rather than east. If Logan were going to venture a guess, he'd say there was a structure of some sort nearby, a place where hiding a vehicle would be easy. A gas station, maybe. Or a rest stop.

He moved cautiously, the sound of interstate traffic mixing with the rustling of leaves and the swish of the wind.

The trees opened into a field of rotting cornstalks. Beyond that, a house jutted up toward the cloud-laden sky. An old farmhouse of some sort. No lights. No sign that the place was occupied. The footprints disappeared into the field, the old husks and tangled plants making it impossible for Logan to find them again.

He followed his gut, heading across the field and straight to the house. An old porch sagged along the front and sides of it, the boarded-up windows and doors speaking of neglect and abandonment. Someone had loved the house once. Now it was simply a place that had once been a home.

Snow blanketed the porch. No footprints there. Logan bypassed the building, moving around to the back of the structure and into an overgrown yard. Still no sign of a vehicle. No footprints. Nothing that would indicate the perp had been there, but Logan could sense something out of place.

He ducked back into the cornfield, crouching low as he moved toward a group of outbuildings clustered near the back of the property. Looked like a couple of sheds and a barn, but it was hard to see through the falling snow. There'd been a driveway once—he *could* see that—the crumbled asphalt just a few feet from the edge of the field.

It didn't look as if it had been used. No tire tracks in the weeds and grass that tangled around chunks of blacktop. Logan wasn't taking any chances, though. He stayed low, stayed hidden, sliding through the darkness the way he'd done dozens of times on dozens of other cases. Set back from the interstate, the property seemed cut off from the world, the hushed tones of the winter storm and the whisper of distant traffic the only sounds.

If he looked, he could find the lights of cars traveling the highway, but he was focused on the mission. The cold, the snow, the wind, all of it ceased to exist as he moved toward the outbuildings.

At first, it was just a hint of something in the air, a chemical scent that brought Logan to a complete stop. He'd nearly been taken out by improvised explosive devices on several occasions, and he recognized the acrid smell of burning electrical wires. He inhaled cold, crisp air and caught a whiff of it again.

He scanned the property and saw a black column of smoke billowing up from the barn. No flames that he could see, but the place *was* burning.

A distraction of some sort?

Didn't matter. Logan had to check it out, make sure that no one was trapped inside the wooden structure. It would go up in minutes, the entire thing devoured by the fire. Someone inside would have limited time to escape.

He pulled out his firearm as he crossed the clearing that separated the field from the barn. At one point, there'd been fencing. Now the old posts lay in piles on the ground.

He moved around to the back of the barn, searching for a window he could climb through. The wide front door would have opened easily, but he didn't plan to be ambushed as he stepped into the structure.

Flames lapped the back corner of the building, the falling snow adding just enough moisture to the old wood to keep the entire wall from being consumed. It would happen eventually. If he was going to enter the building, he needed to move quickly.

He rounded the corner, found a broken window and climbed through. Mice scurried through the rotten hay beneath his feet. A cat yowled from somewhere deeper in the barn. He'd rescue it if he could. After he made sure the perp wasn't hiding in one of the stalls.

His light illuminated bridles and harnesses, old tools, all of it hanging from hooks on the walls. Smoke drifted listlessly through the empty stalls, the open and broken windows sucking it out as quickly as it entered. Whoever had set fire to the barn hadn't poured accelerant inside. A mistake. On a dryer day, the place would already be consumed. Tonight, though, the fire was taking its time. But once it entered the building, it would have plenty of fuel—dry hay, dry walls, dry boards that lay abandoned on the floor.

He stepped over a few, moving toward the front of the barn and the double doors that he could use to escape. His light flashed on piles of hay, bags of food, glowing eyes...

He moved toward whatever was crouched in the corner and saw the kitten that had been yowling. Ugly as sin, its black fur long and matted, one of its ears missing a chunk. He'd seen plenty of barn cats when he was growing up. This one wasn't more than three months old. He expected it to run, but it approached instead, mewing pitifully as it wove through his legs.

He scooped it up and tucked it into the pocket of his coat. His light glanced off more feed bags, a water barrel, a foot. Leg. Body. Nearly hidden by the water barrel and the feed bags. Not a hint of movement. Not a breath.

Dead.

He knew it before he approached, was certain of it before his light flashed across the prone body, the vacant eyes. Shot in the head. Point-blank from the look of things.

Blood stained the guy's jacket, and Logan pulled back the fabric, revealing another bullet wound. This one to the left of the collarbone. A nice, neat little hole, a gunshot wound the guy would have survived. Had survived. The guy's boots were covered in dirt, his pant cuffs wet from snow. Pine needles were stuck in his hair and jutting out of his coat hood.

The perp.

No doubt about it.

He'd made it to what he thought was safety.

And then he'd been killed.

"This does not make me happy," Stella said for what seemed like the hundredth time since they'd left the cabin.

Harper ignored her, her gaze focused on the slushy road, the headlights of her pickup truck splashing across gravel, dirt and snow.

"I know you heard me," Stella pressed, her voice tight with frustration. She wasn't happy with Harper's plan, but short of tying her up and locking her in a closet, there hadn't been a whole lot she could do about it.

Except come along for the ride.

Which she had.

A shame, because Harper would have preferred solitude to Stella's griping complaints.

"It would be difficult not to hear you, seeing as how you've said it a hundred times," she muttered, and Stella laughed.

"I do have a tendency to repeat myself when I feel as if I'm not being heard. It comes from working with an entire team of men."

"You're the only female HEART member?" she asked as she finally reached the main road, pulled onto asphalt and headed toward the old Dillon place. That was where Logan was. Just waiting for Sheriff Hunter to give him a ride back. He'd called Stella to let her know, and Harper had overheard.

She hadn't seen any reason to make him wait. She had a vehicle, and she knew where the Dillon place was. She also knew that the guy Logan had been tracking was dead. She'd gotten that information from one of the deputy sheriffs who had been collecting evidence at the cabin.

"For now," Stella said. "My boss has a sister who wants to join the team. If she can convince her brothers to let her do it, she'll make a good team member."

"That'll be nice for you," Harper said, her gaze fixed on the snowy road and the flakes that drifted lazily in the headlights. The storm had lost most of its strength. If the meteorologist was correct, there'd be rain by morning and just enough warmth to melt whatever remained of the snow.

"We'll see."

"You don't like her?"

"I like Emma fine. I'm just not sure she's cut out for the work. It's a tough job, a dangerous one. She's still a kid."

"A teenager?"

"Twenty-four."

"And you're what? Twenty-five?"

"I'll be thirty in the spring, but I've had a lot

of jobs, done a lot of things. Seen a lot. Emma has been…protected. A lot."

"So maybe it's time for her not to be. A person can't grow up if she's never given the opportunity."

"A great philosophy in theory, Harper, but letting her *grow up* in the kind of work HEART does is a quick way to get her killed. Kind of like you, wandering around when a killer is on the loose."

"The guy is dead, Stella."

"And someone killed him."

"Someone? Logan shot him," she responded, not quite sure what Stella was getting at.

"Not every gunshot wound is fatal. Logan fired a shot that struck the guy, but it wasn't the shot that killed him. Logan said there were two bullet wounds. The second one was point-blank to the perpetrator's head."

Harper hadn't known that, hadn't really taken the time to ask much after she'd heard the guy was dead. She'd assumed that Logan's shot had killed him, and she'd thought the danger was past, that the threat had ended with the man's death.

"You're quiet," Stella said.

"I didn't realize the gunman was murdered."

"He was," Stella said simply. "If you'd asked, maybe you wouldn't have decided you needed to drive out into a storm to rescue someone who doesn't need it."

"Logan was out in the woods for over an hour. He probably does need rescuing," she responded.

"You're ignoring my point."

"Which is?" Harper asked even though she knew exactly what Stella was implying.

"Next time, ask questions so you can have enough information to make a good decision."

"Going to get someone who's nearly frozen is a good decision."

"Not if you're going to die while you're doing it."

"Whoever killed that man is long gone."

"Says the woman who knows nothing about any of this," Stella muttered.

"I know that I'm not going to sit around waiting for other people to fight my battles for me," she replied.

"Great. Good. Wonderful. I just hope that philosophy doesn't get you killed."

"Why would it? No one has any reason to want me dead."

"And yet, people keep trying to kill you."

Truer than Harper wanted to admit.

She needed to find out what was going on. The only way to do that was to talk to Gabe.

He had to know more than she did. Why else would he send someone to find her?

He still hadn't called.

She'd have to go see him, visit his house in DC with all its fancy furniture and girlie decorations. Lydia had had a field day buying things for the house. She'd had her hand in every room except for Gabe's office, and it had showed—gaudy and funky and a little over-the-top.

Just like Lydia.

The thought made her eyes burn and her throat tighten.

She and Lydia had been as different as any two sisters could be, but they'd loved each other.

She sniffed back tears that she wasn't going to let fall, pinched the bridge of her nose, tried hard to think of something other than her sister.

"Things could be worse," Stella said, speaking into the sudden silence, her voice softer than it had been.

"What?"

"They could be worse, Harper. Always, so we just have to make the best of whatever situation we find ourselves in. Like this one." She waved toward the snowy road and the flakes still drifting through the darkness. "We're on the road, probably making ourselves bait for a murderer—"

"That's comforting."

"If you wanted comfort, you should have fired up that wood-burning stove of yours, huddled under one of those nice quilts you have and read a good book," she responded.

"That probably would have been a better plan," she admitted.

"Too late now," Stella responded cheerfully. "You wanted this. You got it, so we'll just enjoy the snow and hope for the best."

Right. Sounded perfect to Harper.

Up ahead, she could see the entrance to the Dillon property—the old gateposts still sticking out of the ground. No gate. Not anymore. It had come down decades ago. At least, that was what she'd heard from people at church. People in Snowy Vista had long memories, and they remembered the way Arthur Dillon had worked the land, sold his produce at local markets, made a good living for himself and his family.

Then he'd died, and his son Matthew had taken over, run the farm into the ground and then left it for greener pastures. No one knew where he'd gone. The old farmhouse had stood empty for two decades, and then a for-sale sign had appeared in the overgrown yard, jutting up from the corner of the crumbling driveway.

That had been two years ago.

As far as Harper knew, the place hadn't even had one showing.

She turned onto the driveway, the truck bumping over deep ruts. She got about a tenth of a mile from the house before she had to stop, a police cruiser blocking her from driving farther. Not from the local sheriff's department. This cruiser was a state police car. Jeb must have called them in. Snowy Vista had a very small police force, and murder wasn't something Harper thought they'd had to deal with much during the history of the town.

She eased the truck off the driveway and parked it in tangled weeds, waiting as a police officer approached. He motioned for her to roll down the window, his face shadowed by the brim of his hat.

"Ma'am, you're going to have to turn around," he said.

"I'm here for a friend of mine," she responded. "Logan Fitzgerald?"

"You're going to have to turn around," he repeated. "No entry to the property by anyone. It's a crime scene."

"I know, but—"

"That's fine, officer," Stella cut in. "Mind if we wait at the mouth of the driveway? Logan was being questioned by Sheriff Hunter, but he's finished now, and we'd like to get him home."

The officer eyed Stella for a moment, then

nodded. "Fine by me, but if I catch either of you out of the vehicle, I'll arrest you."

"No worries. I'm in no mood to spend the night in jail," Stella responded.

That seemed to satisfy the officer.

He walked back to his car, climbed into the vehicle.

"I'm thinking you'd better do what he said," Stella said. "My boss gets any inkling that we're bothering the local PD, and he won't be happy."

"I wouldn't want you to lose your job because of my actions," Harper replied as she backed toward the end of the driveway.

Stella laughed. "Please. Chance wouldn't fire me. He's not that kind of guy. He would lecture me and assign me to desk duty for a month. A fate way worse than being fired, if you ask me." She pulled out her cell phone and texted something. "That should get Logan moving. He's not going to like that we're just sitting here waiting for trouble to find us."

"There are police everywhere," Harper pointed out. She could see them—flashlights moving along the ground, shadowy forms bobbing through the lingering snow.

"And?"

"Whoever killed that guy would be a fool to try something this close to all these officers."

"I'd say most criminals are fools. Smart, but

fools nonetheless. They think they're too intelligent to be caught, too savvy to ever be found out. So they make mistakes. Stupid ones. Like trying to kill a woman who's sitting a few hundred yards from a police cruiser."

"You're assuming whoever did it is still around."

"Statistically speaking, the likelihood that the perp is hanging around watching all the action is pretty high."

Not a pleasant thought.

Harper tried to tell herself that Stella was wrong, that the likelihood was slim to none, but Stella had been at this kind of work for a lot longer than Harper had been shaping clay. It was obvious from the way she moved, the way she spoke, her gritty rough edge that had just a bit of softness beneath it.

Stella knew what she was talking about, and maybe the criminal wasn't the only one who was a fool. Harper had been on her own for a long time. She wasn't used to taking other people's advice. She wasn't really used to being around other people.

She'd been social before, but not eager to have the kind of close and intimate relationships most people longed for. She'd tried it with Daniel, because it had seemed like the thing to do, and because he'd been charming and funny and made her feel like a million bucks.

When that hadn't worked out, she'd been more upset with herself than heartbroken.

She knew how bad her family was at relationships.

She knew how easily fooled they were, how easily taken advantage of, and so she'd made it her goal to be dependent on no one but herself. She hadn't wanted to end up like her mother—wandering from one bad relationship to another. She hadn't wanted to be like Lydia—settling for someone because she was afraid of having no one, of having to do it all alone, provide for everything herself.

She'd wanted something different from that, and she'd gotten it.

Only it hadn't been quite as wonderful as she'd thought it would be. It hadn't been nearly as fulfilling as she'd thought it *should* be. Maybe if Lydia hadn't died, Harper would have changed her tune, made a few deep connections, spent a little more time building relationships and friendships.

She would have liked to believe that was what would have happened. She'd realized after her sister's death that those things were a lot more important than she'd thought.

It would have helped to have them when she'd

been going through the murder investigation. When she'd been the prime suspect in her sister's and niece's murders.

She shuddered, pulling her coat a little tighter.

She had the heat turned up high. It wasn't cold in the truck cab, but *she* was cold, all the memories that she'd tucked away, all the things she tried really hard not to think about suddenly right there at the forefront of her mind.

Something tapped on her window, near her head, and she screamed so loudly, she thought the truck shook with it. Then she realized she was the one shaking.

She turned, expecting…

She didn't know what.

A masked killer, maybe?

A bogeyman come to life?

Instead, she met Logan's eyes. They were black in the darkness, his hair wet from snow. A few flakes shone white against his hair and coat.

"You going to let me in?" he asked, tapping again.

"Right. Sure," she said, her voice trembling as she unlocked the door and scooted to the center of the seat.

Frigid air filled the truck as he climbed in beside her. He looked tired, and he looked angry.

He also looked…good.

She glanced away, uncomfortable with the direction of her thoughts.

She had enough to worry about without adding someone like Logan to the mix.

"How'd everything go?" Stella asked, her voice breaking through the tension.

"About as well as can be expected when the prime suspect is dead," Logan muttered.

"No need to be waspish," Stella replied.

"Waspish?" Logan laughed, the sound gruff and a little hard. "Who uses that word?"

"I do," Stella responded. "Now, how about you tell me what the police found? Evidence? Any clue as to who is responsible?"

"If they'd found that, I wouldn't be sitting in this truck. I'd be out looking for the guy."

"So we're right back where we were a few hours ago," Stella murmured. "No suspects and no working theory as to who might be responsible."

"Exactly. Although, if I had to guess, I'd say the place we should be looking is in DC."

"You think Gabe is involved?" Harper asked, her throat so dry, she barely got the words out.

She didn't want to believe her brother-in-law had killed her sister, but she'd never been able to discount the idea. There'd always been a tiny seed of suspicion. Gabe wasn't afraid to shove people out of his way to achieve his goals. He was aggressive, determined and decisive. If he wanted something, he went after it.

He'd wanted freedom from his marriage.

At least, that was what Lydia had told Harper a few weeks before she'd died—*Gabe asked for a divorce. He said he can't do us anymore.*

She'd laughed when she'd said it, as if the entire thing were a joke. Typical Lydia. She'd never been able to believe that someone could be done with her. She certainly hadn't been done with Gabe. She'd liked his money, his community status, his beautiful home, and she'd had no intention of ever giving that up. Had that gotten her killed?

Had Gabe been desperate enough, frustrated enough, *done* enough to kill her?

FIVE

Bad to worse.

That was the way things had gone, and Logan wasn't happy about it.

He also wasn't happy about the fact that Harper had left the relative safety of her cabin to give him a ride back to her place. A ride he hadn't needed or wanted. A man was dead. Someone had killed him. The person was still at large. It seemed to Logan that the safe thing to do, the smart thing, would have been for Harper to stay behind closed and locked doors until the murderer was found.

Obviously Harper had other ideas.

He glanced at her. She had a beautiful face, an austere profile and a will of steel. The last might be a problem when it came to keeping her safe.

She leaned forward, opening the truck's vents so more warm air poured out. He caught a hint of the outdoors and of something flowery and feminine. That sweet and delicate scent surprised him, because Harper seemed anything but sweet or delicate. She seemed tough and determined, her wiry frame built for running or hiking or lifting buckets of clay and carrying them through the woods.

"You need to warm up," she murmured, shifting in her seat and grabbing a blanket from the truck's extended cab. "A person can get hypothermia quickly out here. Even when the temperature is above freezing."

She tossed the blanket around his shoulders, tugging it into place, her knuckles brushing the underside of his jaw. He felt rough skin and calluses and caught a hint of that scent again.

"I'm fine." He nudged her hands away, ignoring Stella's smirk. "But you might not be if the murderer decides to take a shot at us on the way back to your place."

"I didn't realize there was a murderer when I decided to come out here," she said, a hint of discomfort in her voice. Her gaze jumped from Logan to the window beside him, the darkness beyond it, the night sprinkled with glittering snowflakes. He could almost see her mind working, calculating the risk, estimating the possibility of someone lurking in the shadows, ready to strike. "If I had," she continued, "I probably would have come anyway. I'm a little stubborn like that," she admitted, and something about the way she said it made him smile.

"Admitting it is the first step in recovery," he replied, and she laughed, the shaky sound filling the truck cab.

"Recovery would imply I had a problem that needed to be fixed," she said. "But stubbornness is a strength when you live out in the middle of nowhere."

"You're a braver woman than I am," Stella cut in. "There's no way that I'd live like you do."

She spoke casually, but Logan knew she had an agenda. Stella usually did.

"It's not that scary out here," Harper said, fiddling with the heating vent again. Opening it. Closing it. Opening it.

He touched her hand, stilling the almost frantic movement.

"Depends on your definition of scary," Stella said breezily. "Your cabin is nice, but it's not effective when it comes to staying safe. Too small, for one thing. If someone decided to set it on fire like what happened to that barn, your place would go up in minutes. Then there are the doors and windows. How about we discuss how flimsy they are?"

There it was. Stella's agenda. She wanted Harper out of the cabin and in a safer location. She could join the club. Logan wanted the same thing.

"How about we don't?" Harper replied, but Stella was on a roll. She'd assessed the situation, and she'd come up with a plan to deal with it.

"I could easily kick the front door in. One well-placed foot, and the door would be lying on the floor while you stood there struggling to load your shotgun."

"I have a handgun in my room," Harper said, her voice stiff and tight.

"Let me guess," Stella responded. "It's locked in a box. The clip is locked in a separate box in the office or down in the living room or in one of the kitchen cabinets."

Harper didn't say a word.

Obviously, Stella had hit the nail on the head with that one.

"Do you know how to use the handgun?" Logan asked as he put the truck in drive and pulled onto the slushy road.

"Yes," she muttered. "I know how to use the handgun. I also know how to load the shotgun very quickly. If it's necessary, I can hit a target at twenty yards."

"I'd like to see that," Stella scoffed. She had the least amount of skill with firearms on a team filled with former military and former law enforcement. She was the lone wolf, the only female. She'd earned her right to be there, though. She was a nurse, had trained as a medic in the navy. She knew how to triage patients, how to keep them alive until help arrived. She could hit a moving target if she had to, but there wasn't a person on the team who didn't know how much she'd have hated that.

"And I'd like to see you kick my front door in with one well-placed foot," Harper retorted.

Stella laughed, pulling out her cell phone and texting someone. Their boss wasn't happy with the newest development. He'd been expecting trouble, but Logan didn't think he'd been expecting this much of it.

"You contacting Chance?" he asked, and she snorted.

"Please! The boss has sent me twenty texts asking for updates. I answered one of them."

Great. Those two were on the outs. Again.

They'd dated for about five seconds a few years back, something that had surprised everyone on the team. Logan suspected that it had surprised Stella, because she'd broken things off pretty quickly.

Fear was a powerful motivator, and there'd been plenty of discussion around the office about just how afraid she was. She'd watched her husband die, and that seemed to affect every relationship she had.

Her business. Logan had asked her about it once and she'd nearly cut him off at the knees.

Not a topic he'd broach again. Not because he was afraid of her, but because he was afraid for her. It was her Achilles' heel, and there were times when he wondered if it was going to destroy her.

"Chance will be fit to be tied," he responded, keeping his tone neutral. He didn't like the games Stella played, but he liked her. He also liked Chance. As long as they were civil to each other, he kept his mouth shut.

"Chance is going to be just fine. Knowing him, he's already got a few guys lined up to come out here and help us. Plus, I'm filling Jackson in on things. He'll pass the information to Chance. They're brothers after all. Nearly attached at the hip."

"Not even close, and you know it. Jackson is as likely to tell Chance things as you are."

She shrugged, fluffing her hair as if she couldn't have cared less.

"Don't play games, Stella," he finally said, because he wasn't going to get in the middle of his boss and his coworker, but he couldn't let either of them slow down progress on a case.

"No games, Logan," she said wearily. "I'm just avoiding conflict. Chance and I are like oil and water. We don't mix well, so it's best to keep us separate. He knows it, and he's not going to blow a gasket because I pass information on to Jackson. He's probably already working on getting backup out here, and he's probably already in discussion with the local PD and the DC police."

She glanced at her phone. "Jackson says Chance is sending someone out to escort us back to DC. I told you that Chance would be on top of things."

Logan didn't miss the note of admiration in her voice.

She could say what she wanted, act any way she wanted, but there was no doubt that she had a lot of respect for their boss.

He didn't point it out.

She'd have denied it, and it wasn't his business or his right to argue with her version of the truth.

"Did Chance say who's coming?"

"No. Doesn't matter. Everyone on the team will be an asset."

"What's the ETA?" he asked.

"Four hours." She glanced at her watch. "Should be here a little after midnight."

"They have a safe house ready?" he asked, and Harper tensed.

"I hope," she said quietly, "that you're not thinking I'm going into hiding."

"What we're thinking," he responded, turning onto the gravel road that led to her cabin, "is that you want to stay alive."

"Most people do," she retorted.

"You're not going to do it out here. Not with someone gunning for you. We can protect you from a direct threat—keep intruders out of the house and away from you—but that's not going to do much good if someone tosses a bomb at the cabin or sets fire to the woods surrounding it."

"That would be a major effort in this kind of weather," she said, but the defiance was gone from her voice.

"And it didn't take a major effort to have someone follow Logan to your place?" Stella asked. "To send them gunning for you? It didn't take a major effort to send one of them back to finish the job?"

"You're making a lot of assumptions," Harper murmured. "It's possible—"

"Anything is possible," he cut in. "But that doesn't make it probable or even reasonable. You've been living out here for four years, right?"

"I'm sure that you know I have," she responded, a twinge of bitterness in her voice. "A company like yours doesn't just walk into something unprepared."

"True," he agreed. "We do our homework. You've been living out here for four years without incident. You attend Snowy Vista Community Church every Sunday, and everyone there likes you."

"What'd you do? Spend time in town and ask people about me?" she demanded.

"I spent the night at Dora's place. She's a wealth of information."

"She's the church pianist," Harper said. "And she knows everything she needs to know about everyone in town. Or she thinks she does."

"That was the impression I got." He'd also gotten the impression that Dora was a certified cat lady. A half dozen kittens had been sitting in a basket in his room, and he'd seen another five or six full-grown cats scurrying for cover every time he walked through the hallway.

He frowned, reaching into his pocket, surprised to feel a warm, furry body still there.

"Does Picasso like cats?" he asked as he pulled up to her porch.

"I have no idea. Why?"

He pulled the kitten from his pocket, set it on her lap. It lifted its head and mewed pitifully. "I found it in the barn."

To his surprise, Stella reached for the kitten and lifted it. "A boy. And he's skinny. He also needs a bath. He stinks."

The kitten mewed again, and she sighed, tucking him under her coat. "We can get him fixed up while we make plans. Inside. You want me to check things out, Logan? Or do you want to?"

"Check what things out?" Harper asked.

"The cabin." All the lights were on, every room lit. It looked cozy, warm and inviting, but that didn't mean danger wasn't lurking inside.

"I'll check it out," Logan said. "Shouldn't take long."

He got out of the truck, closed the door and headed up the porch stairs.

Harper should have been the one searching the cabin. She knew every room, every closet, every little hiding spot that someone could fit into.

Not that there were that many of those.

The design was simple and storage space minimal. She'd wanted it that way. No place for all the stuff she'd accumulated before Lydia died. No place to put photographs of the family she no longer had. There was one shelf in her bedroom. She kept a photo of Lydia and Amelia there and a photo of her mother. No photos of Daniel. She didn't need pictures to remember all the ways she'd failed herself in that relationship.

Yeah. The cabin was streamlined. It wouldn't

be difficult for Logan to search. She doubted he'd find anyone. She'd left Picasso in the living room. The dog wasn't the best guard around, but he was a good deterrent.

She still thought she should have been the one searching the place. It was her cabin, her life, her *responsibility*. That was something she took seriously. From the time she was young enough to understand the situation she lived in, Harper had done everything she could to help her mother live up to her obligations. She'd reminded Erica that bills needed to be paid, that food needed to be bought. When she'd gotten a little older, she'd done odd jobs for people, earning money here and there to help pay the bills.

Erica had always appreciated it, and she'd tried to be a good mother.

She really had.

It wasn't that she hadn't wanted to live up to her responsibilities. It was more that she couldn't. She was too caught up in the dramas that she constantly involved herself in. Abusive boyfriends. Cheaters. Liars. There'd been a long string of each throughout the years. In the end, the stress of that had killed her. At least, that was what Harper thought. The official diagnosis had been leukemia.

She frowned. She tried not to think about the past. It was too easy to get caught up in regrets and recriminations. Besides, dwelling in places of unhappiness was the easiest way Harper knew to destroy a life.

"I think I'd better go help Logan," she said, desperate to get out of the truck and do something that would refocus her thoughts, move her out of the place she found herself in much too often—ruminating on all the things that had gone wrong instead of celebrating the things that had been right.

"I think you'd better stay." Stella snagged her wrist, her grip firm.

"It's my house, Stella. My responsibility."

"And you're our responsibility."

"Wrong."

Stella snorted, lifting the black kitten out from under her coat. "We won't argue about it. Not in front of the baby."

She dropped the kitten into Harper's lap, and it meowed pitifully.

A good distraction, and she thought Stella knew it.

"He's probably hungry." She ran her hands over a rough, matted coat. "He's skinny under all this fur."

"He'll fatten up." Stella seemed distracted, her gaze focused on the cabin, then the tree line, then the gravel road behind them.

"You think someone is going to come out

here?" Harper asked, her skin crawling with the thought.

Twice her sanctuary had been breached.

Three times and she didn't think she'd ever call it a sanctuary again.

"It could go either way," Stella responded.

"Meaning?"

"If the guy is smart—and he probably is—he'll stay away for a while, just wait for another opportunity to strike. If he's nuts, he'll be here sooner rather than later."

"I hope he's smart, then."

"I hope he's nuts. I'd rather face him down now, get it all over with, than wait for him to strike again."

"You're assuming that if he comes, we'll be on the winning end."

"I don't ever assume," Stella replied, her voice cold and a little hard. "That would be a sure-fire way to get myself or someone else killed."

"Sorry. I wasn't trying to imply—"

"You don't need to apologize. You didn't say anything offensive. I'm just clearing things up for you, because you've got one of the best teams in the world working to keep you safe. You need to know that, and then you need to do exactly what we're asking you to do."

"We're back to me leaving the cabin and

heading off to some unknown place for an indeterminate amount of time," Harper muttered.

"If it keeps you alive, I don't see what the problem is."

"I have work to do. I've been commissioned—"

"It won't matter if you're dead." Stella cut her off, her gaze focused on the tree line again.

She was right, so Harper didn't respond.

There wasn't anything she could say.

She had a choice to make, and despite what Stella seemed to think—it *was* hers to make. She *could* stay at the cabin, keep the shotgun loaded, the handgun at the ready. She could probably count on Picasso to be an alarm system, or she could pay to have an alarm system put in. She could shore up the windows and the doors, make her quiet retreat a fortress.

Would it be enough?

That was the question she couldn't answer, because she had no idea who was after her or why.

Her cell phone buzzed, and she dragged it from her pocket, glancing at the caller ID.

Gabe. She didn't have his contact information in her phone, but she recognized the number. It was the same one he'd had four years ago.

She answered quickly, knowing he was impatient enough to hang up after the second or third ring. "Hello?"

"Harper? This is Gabe. How are you, kid?"

"I've been better. How about you?"

"Busy. I guess you probably heard that I'm getting married again."

Her stomach dropped, her heart pounding frantically. Married again? It seemed like just yesterday that she'd stood as an attendant at his wedding to Lydia. "No. I didn't."

"I am. You're invited, of course." He cleared his throat, the sound of discomfort surprising. Gabe was always confident, always absolutely sure of himself. "She's a great lady, Harper. I think you'll be happy with my choice."

"I don't see why that would matter. We haven't spoken in four years, Gabe. My opinion is no different than any stranger's would be to you."

"You're wrong," he responded, a hint of sharpness in his tone. "I always liked you, and your blessing matters to me."

Harper didn't know what to say, so she kept silent, waiting for him to continue.

"I think Lydia would approve," he finally said.

"She's dead. She's not going to have anything to say about it one way or another," she pointed out, and he sighed.

"It's been four years. Should I have mourned forever?"

"You didn't even mourn for a day."

"You're wrong, Harper. I loved your sister. I thought we'd have a lifetime together."

There were a dozen things she could have said to that, a few dozen arguments she'd overheard that she could have mentioned, at least two women she could have pointed to, and then there was Lydia's comment about Gabe wanting a divorce. But he was right—Lydia and Amelia had been gone for years. Picking a fight with Gabe wasn't going to change that.

"You went to a lot of effort to find me, Gabe. What do you need?"

"You already know. You mentioned it in the message you left for me. Someone sent me a package. There was a photo of a girl in it. She looked to be about Amelia's age."

"Do you think it's Amelia?" she said, her mouth was dry, her heart thudding.

"I don't know, but I'll do whatever it takes to find out." His voice was cold, more Gabe-like. He'd always been logical to a fault, always handled his fights with Lydia with a detachment that had made his wife seem overly emotional and dramatic in comparison.

"Is there any proof it's her?"

"No, but…" He paused, and she could picture him—chestnut hair cropped close, dark eyes focused. "She looks like a miniature version of

Lydia. Same blond hair. Same green eyes. Same dimple in her left cheek."

Amelia had had a dimple.

It'd peeked out only when she was really happy and really relaxed. Which had been rare. There'd been too much tension in the house, and Amelia had been a sensitive kid.

"Lots of people have blond hair and green eyes. Lots of them have dimples. That doesn't mean—"

"Look." He cut her off, his voice sharp. "I'm not stupid, Harper. I know what the chances are. I spent three days telling myself there was no way the kid in the picture was my daughter. I almost tossed the entire package in the trash and forgot about it. This isn't a good time in my life to be dredging up the past, and I'm not holding out any hope that the little girl is actually my daughter."

"If you feel that way, why did you pay someone to find me?"

"Because my fiancée wouldn't let it go. Even she could see the resemblance. Not just with Lydia but with the photos I have of Amelia."

"Your fiancée looked at the photos?" That wasn't the way Harper had imagined things going. She'd thought for sure that Gabe had packed up every photo of Lydia and their daughter, put them all in a box and stored them somewhere so that he wouldn't have to see them and be reminded of his failures.

"I have photos all over my house," he snapped. "I'm not the ogre your sister painted me to be. I loved her. I made mistakes, sure, but I was trying to fix them."

"By sleeping with other women?" The question slipped out, and she regretted it immediately. Gabe didn't enjoy being backed into corners, and he'd be as likely to hang up and never contact her again as he would be to tell her off.

"I never cheated on your sister."

"The night Lydia died, you were with—"

"A *friend*. Just like I told the police. I wasn't sleeping with Maggie," he bit out. "We were friends long before I met Lydia. Lydia knew that. She said it didn't bother her that one of my best friends was a woman. It did. That was her problem. Not mine."

He sounded sincere, and maybe he was telling the truth.

Harper didn't know. It wasn't her business to care. Not anymore.

"I apologize. It's all in the past, and I shouldn't have brought it up."

"You don't believe me," he said quietly. "And that's fine, but believe this—Maggie was there for me after your sister died and Amelia…

died." He choked the word out. "She helped me through one of the darkest times in my life. A year ago, I realized just how much she meant to me, and—"

"Now you two are going to get married?" she cut in. She didn't want to hear any more about his relationship. She didn't care enough to know. All she wanted was more information on the little girl with the green eyes and Lydia's dimple.

"Yes," he bit out. "Maggie thinks that the girl in the picture could be Amelia. She knew her, and she knew your sister. She pushed me to go to the police with the package, and I did. They sent the photo to the FBI, who ran facial recognition programs on it."

"And?"

"It takes time, and it's only been a week."

"How much longer do they think it will take?"

"Could be a few days or a couple of weeks. It just depends on their workload and how easy it is to run the comparison. There's a big difference between a four-year-old and an eight-year-old. Faces can change a lot in those years."

"I guess they can," she said quietly, because her throat was clogged with emotions she didn't want to feel—anxiety, fear, anticipation. Hope.

That was the big one.

The one she didn't want to hang her hat on.

"I didn't do this to upset you, Harper. I didn't

do it to bring up a lot of hard feelings and ugliness. I did it because I didn't think it was fair to keep you in the dark. You loved Amelia, and if she's alive—"

"I want to know it. Do you have a copy of the photo you can send me?"

"I'll text it to you. Take a little time to look it over. Think about what you want to do. When you're ready, call me again."

He hung up.

Just like that.

Gabe had never been one to waste time.

He'd accomplished his goal. That was all he'd ever really cared about, and maybe that, more than anything, had been the problem between him and Lydia. She'd wanted everything from him—money, jewelry, attention, affection. He'd just wanted to keep living his life, doing his thing with a wife who supported him and made a pretty picture beside him.

Lydia had been a very pretty picture. A beautiful one, actually. But she'd also been needy, clingy and a little desperate.

In the end, they'd never quite worked together. There'd been no team. Just each of them doing what they wanted while the other one complained or fumed. Maybe it hadn't really been either of their faults. Or maybe it had been both of theirs.

Her phone buzzed.

Gabe had already sent the photo.

Her fingers shook as she opened the text, looked at the photo, stared into a face that was so much like Lydia's that her heart nearly broke from looking at it.

"Everything okay?" Stella asked quietly, and Harper nodded, because there was nothing else she could do.

Things weren't okay.

They hadn't been okay in a long time.

She'd done a good job of pretending, she'd created a convincing facade, but her life had fallen apart four years ago. All the plans she'd accomplished since then, all the success she'd had, hadn't done a thing to help her put it back together.

SIX

The cabin was empty.

But then, that was what Logan had been expecting.

The murderer had been down near the old farmhouse. He'd have had to cut back through the woods, bypass any searching K-9 teams and hope to make it to the cabin before he was discovered.

There'd been way too much police presence for that to happen. The murderer might be crazy, but he wasn't stupid. He'd planned out the attacks against Harper, plotted a way to find her, decided how best to accomplish his goals. Whatever those goals might be.

Logan doubted that he'd risk all the work he'd done on a slim chance. He'd wait until things quieted down, until the concern diminished and it seemed as if Harper might be safe. Then he'd strike again.

Logan stepped out onto the back porch and

scanned the clearing behind the cabin. A few narrow saplings jutted up from the earth. Not good cover for anyone who might want to hide. The woods at the edge of the property were thick, though, the large shed that hugged the tree line offering a perfect place for someone who might want to hang around and wait for things to quiet down.

Picasso ran out into the yard, sniffing the ground and the air, excited by all the new scents but not alarmed by any of them. If someone were close by, he'd know it, but he was relaxed.

"Come on, boy," Logan called, and the dog trotted back, his lanky grayish body loping along with unbridled enthusiasm. It had been years since Logan had had a dog. He didn't have time for one. He was gone too much, away from his apartment for too many long stretches of time. If he were someone like Harper, though— home alone most of the time, working in a solitary field that required little to no contact with the outside world—he'd have a dog.

He walked back through the small kitchen, Picasso beside him. A dog dish sat next to a tiny counter that didn't seem big enough to prepare food. The place was…sterile. No clutter. No mugs in the sink. No boxes of crackers or cookies on the counter. A few shelves lined one wall, a couple of pieces of pottery sitting on them. Glazed and painted in shades of blues, greens and yellows, they were the one spot of color in the room.

Harper's work.

He'd done his research. He'd visited a gallery in DC that displayed and sold Ryan Harper's work. He'd seen the price tag on the pieces and watched as a woman had walked in and bought two plates and a mug. A small fortune, but she hadn't blinked an eye.

Ryan Harper had made a name for herself in art circles. There were write-ups in several newspapers and in a few magazines. No pictures of Harper, though. To those who were interested, she was as elusive as Bigfoot.

The living room was as sterile as the kitchen. No personal touches. No photos. No hints of who Harper was. Just a couch. A love seat. A coffee table and an end table. Not a book in sight. Not a magazine within reach. It was as if the place was waiting for someone else to occupy it, as if Harper was just a visitor working hard not to leave her stamp on it.

He filed the thought away. It had no bearing on the mission, wasn't going to add anything to the investigation, but he wanted to think about it more. Maybe because he was thinking about her.

He frowned, jogging outside, the moist air

spearing through his soaked jacket and shirt, chilling his thighs and his soaked feet. He'd forgotten how wet he was, how deep the cold went. His bones felt chilled, his muscles tight in response.

He'd warm up while Harper packed.

And she would be packing, because she would be leaving.

Unless she wanted to be a sitting duck, just waiting for the hunter's bullet.

He reached the truck and opened the door. Harper sat still as stone, the black kitten purring in her lap. If she planned on getting out of the truck and going into the cabin, she wasn't giving any sign of it.

Surprising, since she didn't seem like the kind of person who'd enjoy sitting idle for long.

"The cabin is clear. Let's go," he prodded, taking her arm and helping her from the car.

She felt…solid, the muscles beneath her coat hard and well developed. Not gym muscles. These were muscles honed by hard daily labor, and that intrigued him more than he wanted it to.

He didn't have time for relationships. He didn't have room in his life for someone else. He'd made that decision years ago. As soon as his youngest brother had moved out of the house, he'd offered all three of his brothers the opportunity to take over the farm. Colt had jumped at the opportunity and eagerly thrown himself into farm life. That had freed Logan to do what he wanted, to give up the family life for something more exciting and—for him—more fulfilling. He'd taken the job Chance Miller had offered, moved to Washington, DC, and rented a small apartment there. Two bedrooms. Just enough room to have a guest if he needed to.

Once in a blue moon he'd take his nieces and nephews for a weekend. They'd eat way too many sweets, stay up way too late, watch too much television and play too many video games, and when it was over, they'd go home.

A perfectly acceptable arrangement. One that allowed Logan to be involved without a whole lot of commitment. It fit his lifestyle, suited his personality.

He stepped back into the silent cabin and released Harper's arm. She looked shaken, her face pale, her gaze hollow, the little kitten clutched to her chest.

"You okay?" He touched her shoulder, felt firm muscles again. He wondered about a woman who would give up everything she'd worked for to create something new and uncertain.

"I will be," she responded as she walked to the couch and grabbed a blanket that hung across the back. She tossed it to him, her gaze direct, her eyes a soft, hazy green that reminded him of morning mists and lazy summer afternoons. Something had shaken her, but she seemed to be recovering, forcing herself to go through the motions of normalcy.

He'd seen it before, watched as people who'd been traumatized, abused, injured and devastated moved through the world as if nothing had happened, as if everything was okay.

Survival instinct, he'd always thought.

The need to make it through and go on superseding the desire to cave in and give up.

"You should probably warm up," Harper said, scratching Picasso behind his ears and nudging him down when he tried to sniff the kitten. "There are towels in the bathroom if you want to dry off."

Stella cut in as she walked into the cabin and closed the door. "I think that he would rather get you packed up and out of here."

"We're waiting for your coworker to arrive," Harper responded. No argument about leaving, so Stella had made some progress. "That's going to take a few more hours."

"A few hours that I'd rather not spend here." Stella walked to the front window, pulled the curtains closed. They were sheers. Nothing that would keep someone outside from seeing shadows moving within.

"Is there a better place?" Harper asked, pulling the kitten's claws from her shirt and setting it down on the top edge of the couch.

Logan thought it would run for cover and hide from Picasso. It jumped down instead, wound its way around the big dog's feet and settled into a pile of fur beneath him.

That made Harper smile, and he thought it changed her face, made her look younger than twenty-nine, more vulnerable than she'd seemed before.

"It looks as if they're going to be friends," she murmured as Picasso sniffed the kitten and gave it a gentle lick. "So I guess I'll—" she glanced around "—go pack."

That was it.

She was gone like a flash, running into the kitchen and up the stairs, her footsteps pounding through the small cabin.

"What happened?" he asked Stella, because something had. It had been in Harper's face, and it was in Stella's—tension, unease. Not because of the situation they were in. Stella had faced a lot worse than this.

"Seems as if there's a real possibility her niece is alive. Her brother-in-law just called her. He sent a photo."

"And?"

"Good question. She wasn't talking. I wasn't asking."

"That's not like you."

"It is when someone has been through too much, when they're just on the edge of having had all they can take. I was giving her some time to process things, and then I was going to take a look at the photo. You came out before I got a chance."

"I'll go talk to her."

"Or I could," she offered, eying the dog and kitten. "She might respond better to a woman."

True. She might.

By all accounts, Harper had been a loner for four years, keeping to herself, not making any close friends. She'd closed herself off after her sister's and niece's deaths. Gabe hadn't been able to explain why. He'd just said that she'd packed up her things and left town. No forwarding address, no contact. Nothing for four years. According to her brother-in-law, Harper's actions were out of character. She was one of the most responsible people he'd ever met, and Gabe hadn't seen any reason for her to run.

Logan had. He'd read the newspaper accounts of the murder investigation. Harper had been a prime suspect for nearly a month, her motives scrutinized by every reporter in DC. Thanks to Gabe, who'd been more than happy to fan the flames.

That had struck Logan as interesting.

The guy must have known he was next on the list of suspects. Even with his airtight alibi.

"I don't think she's going to be responsive to either of us," Logan said. "So I may as well be the one to talk to her."

"Suit yourself," Stella responded with a shrug. "I'm going to call Jackson, see who his brother sent out."

"His brother's name is Chance," he said, poking her a little, and she scowled.

"I'm well aware of that."

"I figured you were, but since you avoid saying his name as if the sound of it will poison your ears—"

"I don't avoid anything," she spit out, her eyes blazing.

"Right, because avoidance is for cowards," he agreed, quoting one of the things he'd heard her say dozens of times.

She blinked, some of the fire leaving her eyes, and offered a sheepish smile that made him realize she was just a human being, not the superhuman creature she always seemed to be when they were on a mission together.

She'd been through her own traumas and heartaches, and she'd come out of them stronger. Whatever the thing was with Chance, whatever her response, it wasn't Logan's business to prod the wound.

"Stella," he began, wanting to apologize, tell her that he should have kept his big mouth shut.

"Go talk to her. Find out what's got her so shaken up. We have to plan our next step. We can stay here and wait for backup, or we can move her to another location and wait there," she cut in, every word precise and practical, her focus shifted back to the job.

Stella the superhuman again, and he had about three seconds to wonder what she was like beneath the hard-won facade before she shooed him away.

"Hurry up, Logan. We've got danger breathing down our necks, and we're out in the middle of nowhere. If something goes down, escaping it might not be all that easy. I don't know about you, but I'd rather not get into a blazing gun battle in the middle of rural Maryland."

He nodded and headed toward the back of the cabin.

The stairs creaked under his weight as he made his way to the upper level of the cabin. At one time, it had probably been a loft—a simple storage space or a small room that opened into the main area below. The floor had been stretched out, the various lengths of hardwood that had been used to finish it oddly beautiful. None of them matched, and he thought Harper must have salvaged pieces from condemned properties or maybe visited junkyards to collect what she'd used to finish the cabin.

She had an artist's eye. That made the lack of decor, the plain white walls and empty shelves all the more incongruent.

A small room sat at the top of the stairs, a doorway beyond leading into Harper's room and the tiny bathroom that jutted off it. He'd been through every inch of the cabin. He knew the layout, could picture the large windows that looked over her backyard.

Hopefully she wasn't anywhere near them.

He knocked on the door and thought he heard a muffled response.

He knocked again. "Harper? We need to talk."

The door swung open, and she appeared. She'd changed into dark jeans and a sweater that still had the tag hanging from the sleeve. She snapped it off, crumbled it, tossed it into a small plastic garbage can that sat near the bathroom door.

"This is one of my go-to-town outfits, only I never actually wore it," she explained, stepping back so that he could move into the room.

A small duffel sat in the center of the bed, a few pieces of clothing spilling out of it.

"I thought we were going to have a debate about the merits of you leaving the cabin," he commented. "I guess I was wrong."

"No debate, Logan. I'm leaving, and I'm heading back to DC. I want to speak with Gabe."

That wasn't the plan.

The plan was that she'd go to a safe house and stay there while people a lot more suited to the work than she was searched to find answers.

"About?"

She pulled out her cell phone and thrust it toward him. "See the little girl?"

She would have been difficult to miss. The girl was front and center. Maybe a copy of a school photo, the background plain white, the girl fair with green eyes. No smile, and the jaunty bows someone had wrapped around her pigtails only made that more obvious. "What about her?"

"She looks like my sister."

"There are lots of people in this world who look like other people, Harper," he said gently, because he knew where this was going, knew what she must be thinking.

Or wanting.

Hoping?

That was the path he'd been down dozens

of times after his father's body was found. Every hazy photo snapped by a tourist or security camera, every word-of-mouth account of a foreign woman traveling with nationals had sparked a hope that his mother might be alive and a dream of pursuing the lead to the ends of the earth in an effort to find her.

"I know," she responded, shoving the clothes the rest of the way into the duffel and grabbing a small black Bible from the bedside table. She had a minimalist approach to decorating. The same seemed to be true of packing. Either that or she didn't plan to be gone long. She zipped the bag, hefted it on her shoulder. "I'm heading out."

"We should probably talk about things first." He was standing between her and the door, and he didn't move. He'd never been a bully, never believed in throwing around his weight, height or muscles. If she wanted to leave, he wasn't going to stop her, but he wasn't letting her go alone. She might as well know that, and she might as well spend a little time planning things out so that she didn't walk into a trap or into gunfire.

"What things?" She walked to one of the few photos displayed in the house. He'd looked at it when he'd walked through. He'd seen it before. In Gabe's office when he'd gone there to discuss the case, feel the guy out, see why he suddenly wanted to find a sister-in-law he hadn't seen or heard from in years.

"How you're going to go visit Gabe and stay safe, for one."

She shrugged, her gaze focused on the photo—the beautiful blond woman dressed to the nines, her hair done up, her makeup flawless, a little girl beside her. Also blond, her hair just long enough for tiny pigtails on the sides of her head, the child couldn't have been more than two years old. Like her mother, she was beautiful. Would have grown into a beautiful woman if she hadn't died.

Disappeared?

That would be a twist in the story, a hiccup in a job that he'd thought would be a straightforward missing-persons search.

Only Harper hadn't really been missing.

If Gabe had taken the time, he'd have found her.

That left a bad taste in Logan's mouth and a bad feeling somewhere in the region of his stomach.

Things felt off, and they obviously were. Otherwise, he'd have found Harper, she'd have told him to go away and he'd have left. Mission accomplished, case complete, time to move on to something else.

Harper slid the photo into the duffel. "I can't stay hidden forever."

"It won't be forever."

"Who's to say? We plan all kinds of things. We think that we have life figured out, that the path we've set for ourselves is the one we're going to stay on. Then something comes along and blocks our way, and we have to head in new directions, make new decisions based on new information. Gabe sent me the photo on my phone. It was mailed to him with a piece of cloth that looked like part of Amelia's blanket."

"That doesn't mean she's Amelia," he said, keeping his tone light and his words as neutral as possible.

He didn't know if the girl was Amelia.

If it was, if she was alive, they'd find her.

He couldn't make that promise to Harper, though. Not yet. Not until he spoke with Chance, got his approval to expand the scope of the case, take on some things they weren't being paid for. Unless Gabe decided he wanted more than his sister-in-law found. Maybe he'd hire HEART to search for his daughter.

That was a possibility that excited Logan, a case that wasn't cut and dry and easy. If Amelia was alive, she'd been hidden well for four years. There'd be no paper trail, no way of tracking her. No clues. No people to interview. The last person to see her was dead.

He studied the image on the cell phone, the wide-set eyes, the perfect arch of the brows. The girl couldn't have been older than eight, but she had a maturity to her face, a stunning beauty that people would notice and remember. That kind of beauty was reflected in every photo he'd seen of Lydia, and he'd seen plenty of them. He'd pored over newspaper articles, tried to get a sense for what had happened, how a woman who'd had everything, had seemed to be loved by everyone who knew her, had ended up dead.

"You're quiet," Harper said, her arms crossed over her stomach. She had a more subtle beauty than her sister. Light green eyes instead of bright green. Soft brown hair instead of blond. Nothing flashy in her face or in her actions, and yet, there was something compelling about her, something interesting. He wanted to study her face, try to figure out what it was that made him want to look and keep looking.

"Just thinking that things aren't what they seemed when my boss agreed to help your brother-in-law find you, and that if your niece is alive, I'd like to be part of bringing her home."

"If she's alive."
The words didn't quite roll off Harper's tongue.

They didn't quite settle in her brain.

Maybe because she wanted so badly for them to be true. She wanted so desperately to believe that the police had been wrong, that Amelia hadn't been killed, that somehow she'd survived the night Lydia died and that she still survived.

Alive. Somewhere.

She had to talk to Gabe again, get more information on the new investigation. If Amelia was alive…

Was she okay?

Happy?

Scared?

Wondering why she'd been abandoned by the people who loved her?

She took the cell phone from Logan's hands, her fingers brushing warm, rough flesh. She could feel the weight of his stare as she scrolled through old photos that she'd uploaded to her phone. She found a picture of Amelia the last time they'd been together. Ice cream on her chubby cheeks, a bow listing to the side of her fine blond hair.

She had been adorable and precocious, already reading fluently by the age of four. Lydia had been talking about moving her from the Montessori preschool she'd been attending to a classical school on the outskirts of Alexandria.

So many opportunities had been open to

Amelia. She'd had every advantage, and Lydia had been proud of that.

It hadn't been enough to keep either of them safe.

All the money in the world hadn't been able to keep Lydia alive.

Harper blinked back tears, the hot burning pain of them surprising. It had been a lot of years since she'd cried over her sister's and niece's deaths, a lot of years since she'd woken in the middle of the night, bathed in sweat, her sister's pale, still face filling her head.

She'd been the one to identify Lydia's body.

Gabe had claimed that he couldn't do it, that he didn't want his last memory of Lydia to be of her lying on a steel gurney.

The truth was, he was a coward. He wanted his life sterile and safe, no messy emotions or overblown drama. Lydia was supposed to be his trophy wife, the beautiful woman who'd accompany him to gala functions and meetings with high-profile clients.

She'd been too emotional for him, too unpredictable.

Maybe that was why things had ended the way they had.

"Harper?" Logan's hand cupped her elbow, as if he thought she might fall over without some support.

"I'm okay."

"Sure you are."

"I will be okay," she responded. "Is that better?"

"It's more honest, and it's correct. You will be okay."

"And I *will* go to Gabe's. I have to talk to him. I want to see the piece of cloth he received in the mail, see if it matches the one I have."

"Did you pack that?"

She nodded. She'd grabbed it first, keeping it in the envelope it had arrived in and stowing it in the bottom of the duffel. She'd thought about packing just that. She didn't care about preparing for days or weeks or worrying about whether or not she'd have enough to sustain her until she could return. All she wanted to do was talk to her brother-in-law and see if the things they'd been sent matched. If his little piece of blanket was the same as hers, if they'd both been pulled into something neither of them had known anything about.

Only, she wasn't certain that Gabe hadn't known.

As much as she hadn't wanted to suspect it, as much as she'd told herself that everything Gabe had done had been to protect his reputation and keep him from losing clients and credibility, she'd always wondered if he'd thrown her under the bus to keep suspicion focused in other directions.

"What else do you need?" Logan prodded, and she realized she was standing there, the duffel over her shoulder, her heart beating frantically, the tears so close to the surface she was afraid they'd fall.

"Answers."

He nodded. "Let's go get them, then."

"Just like that?"

"What did you expect?"

"An argument for your plan?"

"My plan is to keep you safe and to help you find out the truth about your niece."

"I'm not sure that Gabe is going to be happy to have you involved."

"Why wouldn't he be? He hired HEART. He's the one who got me involved."

"He got you involved in finding me, but that doesn't mean he wants you to stay involved. Gabe likes to be in charge, and he likes things done his way. He won't be happy if you stir the pot and mess things up."

"If he's not, then it's because he has something to hide, something that he'd rather not have come to light."

"I was thinking that," she murmured. She was thinking a lot of things, and she wasn't comfortable with most of them.

She'd spent four years believing her niece was dead, four years certain that she had no family, no obligations, no need to be anywhere other than where she wanted to be—safe and secure in the cabin.

If Amelia was alive, everything changed.

If Amelia was alive, Harper would go back to DC.

If she was alive, then that was something Harper needed to know, something she desperately needed to find out. *Now.* Not two days from now or a month from now.

Her pulse jumped at the thought, the need to find the truth making her want to run straight to Gabe's place. There was no room for concern about her own safety, no time to think about whether or not she'd put herself in more danger if she visited her brother-in-law.

"You can't avoid looking at me forever," Logan said quietly, and she realized that was exactly what she'd been doing. Avoiding his midnight blue eyes, his handsome face, the truth she knew she'd see in his gaze.

He had no vested interest in her, but he'd taken a job, and he'd see it through to the end.

Whatever that end might be.

She didn't know how she felt about that, but the room was small, and he was close. If she let herself, she could imagine coming out on the other side of this new problem, this new trial, with someone standing beside her. Someone a little stronger than she was, a little more certain of his place in the world.

She wouldn't let herself.

Shelby women never chose well. Not when it came to men. Harper had made a mistake with Daniel. She'd believed his promises and his lies, and she'd had her heart broken because of it.

She wouldn't repeat that mistake. She'd never again allow herself to rely on someone else, to depend on that person.

That was the way to heartache, and Harper figured she'd had enough of that to last her a lifetime.

SEVEN

They waited for Logan and Stella's coworker because that made more sense than running off foolishly into the storm.

By the time Malone Henderson arrived at the cabin, the sky had cleared, moonlight filtered out onto the glistening yard and Harper had studied the picture of the little girl for so long, her eyes hurt and her head ached. All the studying in the world hadn't given her a clear answer about whether or not the girl was Amelia. She needed to talk to Gabe, to Detective Willard, to the FBI. She wanted to know what law enforcement was thinking. More than anything, she wanted to know the truth.

She shivered as she walked to Malone's SUV. Any other night, Harper would have filed away the loveliness of the ice-coated ground, the glittering trees, the moonlight sparkling in the trees. She'd have shoved them deep into that place where she collected images of things she wanted to create—the beauty of the natural world, the vibrant colors of creation. She'd always loved those things. When she'd been a graphic designer in DC, she was known for her bold approach. Rich colors, sharp angles, clean, crisp designs that jumped out at the viewer. Now she preferred subtlety. The soft color of the sky at dawn, the deep oranges and reds of the leaves at the very end of fall, the swirl of wind through trees, the gurgle of water over pebbles—those were the things she tried to capture now.

"In," Malone said as he opened the SUV's door. Just that one word spoken in a gruff and impatient voice. It was enough to get her moving quickly. She slid into the SUV, stopping in the center of the bench seat as Logan urged Picasso into the back of the vehicle and set the kitten in with him.

Simple.

Easy.

Everything going the way all three HEART members had told her it would. She'd been given a blow-by-blow, minute-by-minute detailed account of how they were going to leave the cabin. She'd followed instructions to a T because she didn't want to waste time, and because it all made sense—the caution, the procession of armed people guarding her as they walked across the yard. Even Malone made sense. The guy was huge, taking up way more than his fair share of the backseat. The scar that bisected his left cheek and slid toward his jugular only added to the menacing picture he made.

If she'd seen him on the sidewalk in the middle of broad daylight, she'd have taken a wide path around him.

If she'd seen him at night, she'd have turned and walked the other way.

Or run, because the guy was packing heat, and he wasn't hiding it. His gun was clearly visible, strapped to his chest and announcing that he was ready for whatever might come.

Nothing did.

Logan tossed Harper's bag in with the animals and rounded the car.

She thought he'd get in the front seat, but he opened her door and slid in beside her.

"You could sit next to Stella," she muttered.

She did not, by any stretch of the imagination, want to be sandwiched between Logan and Malone.

"It's a better idea to keep someone between you and whatever might be on the other side of the glass," Logan said, his fingers brushing her hip as he buckled his seat belt.

Just a light touch, a fleeting brush of warmth, but it lingered as Stella pulled away from the cabin.

Harper had turned off all the cabin lights. Everything was dark. She caught a glimpse of the studio, the shed glistening in the moonlight.

It felt final. As if she were saying goodbye for the last time, and she wondered if she'd come back to stay, or if she'd pack up and leave, sell the place and move on. She loved the cabin, the woods, the creeks that splashed through the property. She loved the silence, the solitude, but that had been taken away. Even if she returned, things wouldn't be the same. She'd been found, and she couldn't go back to the anonymity that she'd worked so hard for.

Logan leaned close, his breath ruffling the hair near her ear as he whispered, "Relax."

"I am relaxed," she said, but they both knew she wasn't. Her muscles were taut, her back ramrod straight. To her left, Malone sat silently, his face turned to the window, his expression unreadable.

To her right…

Logan.

He wasn't as broad as his coworker, but he was just as packed with muscle, his shoulder and arm pressed against hers. She shifted, then realized she'd moved closer to Malone. He muttered something under his breath, and she shifted again. She was uneasy. Uncomfortable.

With the men. With the people. With the tension that seemed to fill the car.

They were expecting trouble.

She had no doubt about that.

Would they get it?

That was something she wasn't as certain of.

She wanted to believe that the person who'd come after her was long gone, that maybe he'd fulfilled his agenda and would leave her alone. She might even be able to convince herself that it was true. Believing a lie never changed anything, though. She'd believed plenty when she was dating Daniel. Mostly because she'd wanted to. Daniel had been handsome and charming. He'd bought her flowers and taken her to art exhibits and symphony concerts. He'd told her that she was everything he'd ever wanted, everything he'd been asking God for.

She nearly snorted at the memory.

She'd been pulled in, hook, line and sinker. Until she'd gone to his apartment to surprise him with a home-cooked meal and found him entertaining another woman.

The SUV rounded a curve in the road, and her muscles tightened. She did not want to fall into either of the men.

"If you sit like that the entire trip to DC," Logan murmured in her ear, "your muscles are going to lock up and you won't be able to get out of the car."

"I'll cross that bridge when I come to it," she muttered, because there was no way she planned to lean against him or against his co-worker. Her only other option was to just keep on doing what she was—sitting as straight and tense as she could.

"We'll have to cross it together, because if you can't get out, I'm going to have to carry you. That could get a little awkward."

"Not much more awkward than sitting between two men I don't know," she responded, but she forced herself to relax, to release the tension in her neck and her back.

He chuckled, his attention on the window or the darkness beyond it.

Just like Malone. Both of them seemed completely focused and completely relaxed, but the tension was there, filling the silence, pulsing around Harper like a living thing.

She wanted to talk. Just to fill the silence. But there'd been so many years of being alone, of having no one but herself and God to communicate with, that she wasn't sure what to say, how to begin.

"I've been thinking about your brother-in-law," Stella said, breaking the silence and saving Harper from having to do it.

"What about him?"

"He was prime suspect in your sister's murder. And your niece's. Although if Amelia is alive..." She shrugged, her hair a deep burnished red in the dashboard lights. "I guess he couldn't be a suspect in that."

"He could be a suspect in her disappearance, though," Malone cut in. "A guy like that...lots of money, lots of women, lots of power. Maybe he got tired of his wife, but she wasn't tired of him. Maybe he wanted her out of his life for good, but he didn't have the heart to kill his own kid."

"Malone," Logan said, his voice sharp and a little hard. "Let's not make presumptions, and let's remember that this is Harper's family we're talking about."

"Family stands together, man. They don't break apart when things get tough. Gabe Wilson isn't family," Malone commented.

"Lydia Wilson was," Logan said firmly, and that was it.

End of the conversation, but Harper didn't want it to end. She wanted to hear more about what Stella was thinking, what she'd learned.

She cleared her throat, tried to get the emotion out and the facts in. "I was a prime suspect, too. I'm sure if you read the police report, you know that. As far as I remember, they weren't investigating Gabe."

"You were a person of interest, and that was only because you were the last person to see your sister and niece alive," Stella corrected her as they bounced over a deep rut in the road, then stopped at the entrance to the freeway. A few cars crawled by, lights splashing on the wet pavement. It was still icy, still dangerous. Maybe that would keep the killer away.

"That's not the way I remember things," Harper replied.

"What do you remember?" Logan's gaze was still focused outside the SUV, his arm and shoulder pressed against hers.

She could have moved, but it would only have called attention to her discomfort, and there was nothing to be uncomfortable about. They were on their way, heading to Gabe's and the answers she needed.

Simple as that.

Only nothing seemed simple.

"There were a bunch of newspaper stories about me. I was portrayed as a jealous younger sister who'd wanted everything her sister had."

"Was it true?"

"Maybe from Gabe's perspective. He told the police that I was jealous of Lydia's marriage and her happiness."

"Were you?" Stella asked as she turned onto the country road that led to town. From there, they'd connect to the interstate and head south toward Maryland.

"No. I had a great job. Good friends."

"And you'd broken up with your boyfriend a couple of months before," Stella pointed out. As if it mattered. As if that had been a reason for her to be jealous of her sister.

"Nearly a year before that. Not that it matters," she said, her back already aching from sitting up straight.

She wanted to lean back against the seat, but she was afraid the bumpy country road would send her flying into Malone or, worse, Logan.

"I read the police reports. Your brother-in-law mentioned that to the police. More than once," Stella continued. "I guess he was trying to make it seem important."

"Gabe had his own agenda, I guess."

"To get you tossed in jail?" Stella asked.

"Or to keep himself out of it," Logan responded.

"He wasn't doing a very good job of that," Stella said. "According to a friend of mine who works for DCPD, Gabe was a few pieces of vital evidence away from being charged with your sister's murder."

"I…had no idea," Harper admitted. "Gabe told me to get a lawyer. He warned me that I was in deep trouble."

"And you believed him?" Malone muttered. "Why? Because he'd proved to be a great husband and father? An upright guy who'd loved his family?"

"Because I was being questioned by the police on a daily basis. The newspaper stories were everywhere, and people were looking at me as if I was a card-carrying member of the kill club. Clients stopped requesting me. My boss reassigned me to less prestigious projects. Eventually, he said the bad press wasn't good for his company, and he let me go," she replied, her voice shakier than she wanted it to be.

Too many memories. None of them good ones. She'd have preferred now to make the trip in silence, but burying her head in the sand wasn't going to help her find the truth.

"It was a tough time," Logan responded, and she wondered if he really understood just how tough it had been. She'd lost her sister and her niece. Then she'd lost her job, given up the home she'd loved, the few friends she'd had.

"It was, but I made it through." She'd make it through this, too. She'd meet with Gabe, see what he had to say, talk to the police, decide on a plan of action. She *was* going to act. If Amelia was alive, she planned to find her. No matter what danger it put her in. She owed her sister that. She owed Amelia that. She owed it to herself, too. She couldn't live with not knowing. She couldn't go back to what she'd been doing and pretend that she didn't have doubts, that she wasn't wondering if the young girl in the picture Gabe had sent her was Amelia.

She leaned her head back against the seat and closed her eyes. She was done talking about the past. Until she saw Gabe, there wasn't much more that could be done. Her fingers itched to pull the cell phone from her pocket, scroll through to that photo again. She left the phone where it was, kept her eyes closed. Let Logan think she was asleep, let Stella keep driving and Malone keep staring silently out the window. She had a lot to think about, a lot to plan. One way or another, she had to find the truth. She'd risk anything for that. Even her life.

Harper was a loose cannon.

Logan had dealt with his fair share of them over the years. Hostages who thought they knew better than the team member who was trying to rescue them, desperate families willing to risk anything to have a loved one returned, men and women who thought they had a better plan, a better idea, a more secure way of getting things done than HEART. They'd all been wrong, and they'd all caused plenty of trouble. Generally, things worked out okay because HEART members were well trained and professional. They knew how to prepare for any eventuality, and they never went into a situation without more than one method of getting out.

That didn't mean he liked dealing with the mavericks. They made things difficult. Unless he missed his guess, Harper was going to do the same. Eyes closed, every muscle tense, she sat silently as Stella drove through Snowy Vista.

The small town had bedded down for the night, lights off in the houses, businesses closed. Even the local bar had turned off its sign. Stella sped through a green light, eased off the gas as she approached the sheriff's department. The sheriff's car was parked in front of it.

"Want to stop in for a visit?" Stella asked. "See if the sheriff has ID'd the perp who shot at you earlier? Maybe they've found that car, too."

"No," Logan and Harper answered in unison.

She didn't open her eyes, but her lips twitched.

"Jinx," she murmured, and he smiled.

"Sorry. I stopped playing that game when my last brother went off to college."

"You have a lot of brothers?" she asked, finally opening her eyes. They looked black in the darkness, her lashes long and thick. She'd pulled her hair up into some kind of loose bun, and thick curly strands fell against her neck.

She was a beautiful woman. More interesting than conventional. He didn't think she knew it, though.

"Three. I raised them after my parents died. Finished raising them, I guess you could say. The youngest had just started high school." That was more than he usually told people, but then, he didn't normally give people a chance to ask questions. The women he dated? They were like him—more focused on career than on relationships. They were happy to have a meal or two with him, see a movie, maybe go hiking or rock climbing. Other than that, they were content to do their own thing. That was the way Logan liked it.

"It must have been tough," Harper said, and he shrugged. It had been tough, but he wasn't going to say that in front of Malone or Stella. They'd all been through tough times, and none was any more likely than another to rehash the difficulty.

"We muddled through. I made sure all three finished college. That's what my parents would have wanted."

"And then?" she prodded.

Maybe she wanted a distraction. Something to keep her mind from going where he knew it must be—her niece. A little girl presumed dead four years ago.

If she was alive, that changed everything.

Harper had to know that.

She had to be thinking about it, and maybe she didn't want to.

Hope was a double-edged sword. It kept a person going, but also kept him searching for something that might not ever be found. Logan had been there. Done that. He'd spent a long time thinking he could bring his mother home. That somehow, somewhere, she was still alive, still waiting for rescue. It had taken nearly a decade for him finally to let go of that hope. The fact was, he wasn't certain he ever truly had. He'd just learned to live with the tiny bit of doubt, the little niggling thought that maybe if he just tried a little harder, searched a little longer, pushed a little further...

He shoved the thought away, turned his attention back to the conversation. Distraction was something he could offer Harper. It wouldn't do her any good in the long run, but for the ride to DC, it would help her relax, keep her from dwelling on things she couldn't change.

"After I got my brothers through college, I joined HEART."

"And the world is a better place for it," Malone intoned.

Stella snorted. "Moody much, Malone?"

"That was a sincere compliment. If I'd been going for sarcasm, I would have changed the tone of my voice."

"The tone of your voice changes? I thought growls were the only thing you could manage," Stella retorted.

"Growls are effective in getting points across, and right now my point is this—I want to get back to DC. I've got some things to take care of."

"Things?" Stella echoed.

"Yeah. *Things.* Thanksgiving is around the corner, and I've got a big meal I'm planning."

"For whom? You have family coming into town?" It was a good question, and Logan was curious to hear the answer. As far as he knew, Malone didn't have family. He lived alone in an apartment just outside DC. He had no pets. No plants. Nothing that required any amount of time or attention. Logan only knew because he'd brought Malone home from the hospital after he'd nearly been killed by a sniper bullet while he was working a case in Turkey. He'd spent two weeks in a hospital there, one week in a hospital in Alexandria. When he'd been released, he'd asked Logan to bring him home.

That was the first and last favor he'd ever asked.

Logan got the impression that he wasn't the kind of guy who ever wanted to owe anyone.

"You're nosy today, Silverstone," Malone muttered.

"How is asking a few questions nosy?" Stella demanded, and the next thing Logan knew, the two were bickering like old fishwives.

That was fine.

They tended to butt heads, but they worked well together. If there was a problem, they'd have his back and each other's. That was all that mattered.

Harper shifted beside him, her eyes closed again, a soft smile curving the corners of her lips. She looked younger, more vulnerable than she had when he'd first seen her.

"Good memories?" he asked, his breath ruffling her hair.

The smile fell away, and she met his eyes. "Just thinking about the way my sister and I used to bicker. We'd fight over nothing and everything, but we always came back together in the end." She paused. "Until we couldn't. It's funny how we always think we're going to have another day with someone, another opportunity to tell her how much she means to us. We think there's going to be a tomorrow, but there isn't always."

"I'm sorry," he said, because there was nothing else he could say. He'd lived through all the tired platitudes after his parents were kidnapped. He'd heard them a million times—*I'm praying. God is in control. Your parents would want you to go on. Things will work out the way God wants them to.*

The last had always been the hardest to take, because he couldn't believe that God wanted any family to be destroyed, that He wanted anyone to suffer.

"Thanks," she responded, her hands fisted in her lap.

"I know it doesn't help," he continued, and she smiled again. This time, the expression was sad rather than gentle.

"It's better than a million words designed to make the speaker feel better."

"I'm sure you've heard all of them."

"I'm sure you have, too." She rubbed at a spot on her jeans. It looked like a daub of paint, but she seemed determined to remove it. "Did they die together?"

He didn't have to ask what she meant. She'd circled back around to his comment about raising his siblings. His knee-jerk reaction was to sidestep the question. It was what he'd usually have done. The subject was a tough one, the pain still real even after so many years.

"I don't know," he said, surprising himself

with the honesty. It wasn't something he talked about. Not even with his brothers. "They were on a short-term mission trip when they were kidnapped. My father's body was found a few days later. My mother was never recovered. That's probably the hardest part. The not knowing. That's why I joined HEART, to give other people the closure I've never had."

"It's my turn to say that I'm sorry."

"It was a long time ago, Harper."

"Does that make it hurt less?"

"It makes the hurt a little easier to bear," he responded, and she nodded.

"I guess that's true. Today, though, all the hurt seems fresh and new."

"Because you think your niece is alive." It wasn't a question, but she nodded.

"It brings everything to the fore, makes me question everything that happened back then. I wish…"

"What?" he asked, and she smiled that sad smile again.

"That it wasn't another hundred miles to DC."

"We're not going to DC yet. We'll head to the safe house first," Stella cut in. "The boss is getting it ready. He's using that place in Davidsonville. Remember it, Logan?"

He remembered. An old farmhouse in the middle of nowhere. It was large and unremarkable. Unless a person looked closely enough. Then he'd notice the security cameras, the ten-foot fence, the gate that opened with a code. Inside, it was comfortable and updated, a good place to spend a few hours after a very long day and night, but he didn't think that was part of Harper's plan.

She stiffened. "I thought we agreed that we were going to see Gabe."

"It will be two in the morning when we reach DC. I don't think he's going to appreciate a visit at that time of the night."

"I don't think I care," Harper responded.

"And I don't think it's up to you." Stella glanced in the rearview mirror, her face pale in the dashboard light. She looked tired, and that worried Logan. Stella was never tired, never out of energy. Tonight, though, she looked done in.

"You're wrong." Malone chose that moment to reenter the conversation. "It *is* up to her. She's under no obligation to do things our way. Of course, if she messes up and ends up keeping us from finding her niece, that's on her, too."

"Smooth," Harper muttered, pulling her knees to her chest and wrapping her arms around them.

"Hey, I'm just stating a fact. The other fact I'd like to state is this—she's right about going to see Gabe Wilson at an unexpected time. From what I can gather, the guy has an answer for everything. If we give him enough time, he'll figure out a way to twist every fact to benefit himself."

"He's had four years to plan every word he wants to say," Logan pointed out, but he was anxious to speak to the guy, too. They'd met a couple of times before HEART had agreed to take the case, and Logan had felt confident the guy was on the up-and-up.

Now he wasn't so sure.

Gabe Wilson was getting married in a couple of months. His fiancée was the daughter of a well-known career politician, but she was accomplished in her own right—a pediatric neurologist with a great reputation. The press loved her. The community loved her. Wilson apparently loved her. The last thing he'd want was a rehashing of old drama. Maybe he'd been afraid Harper would hear about the engagement and make accusations about his involvement in her sister's and niece's murders. Maybe he'd been determined to keep her from ruining his chances of marrying into money and political clout.

Maybe...

But Logan was usually spot-on about people, and he didn't think Gabe Wilson was calling the shots on this attack on Harper. Did he know who was? That was something Logan needed to find out.

"I'm going to DC," Harper announced. "I don't care if I have to walk there."

Stella shrugged as if she didn't care one way or another, but the tightness of her jaw said something different.

"Suit yourself," she said. "Better text the boss and let him in on the new plan," she tossed out as she merged onto the interstate and headed south toward DC.

EIGHT

It had been four years, but Harper hadn't forgotten the posh elegance of Gabe Wilson's home. Lydia's home, once upon a time, and she'd been so proud of that. Harper could remember her sister's excitement, the way she'd pored over catalogs and walked through department stores. The house had been Gabe's bachelor pad, but Lydia had been determined to put her feminine touch on everything. Now nothing of Lydia remained. No bright-colored flowers in a vase on the mantel. No faux-fur throw rug. No pink velvet chaise longue.

"You okay?" Logan asked, his large frame blocking her view of the pocket doors that opened into the hall. It was for the best. There were too many memories there, hidden in photos and collages and framed paintings made by toddler hands. Harper had been surprised when the housekeeper had led them to the sitting room and asked them to wait. Gabe had known they were coming. She'd had to call him for the code to the community gate, and she'd thought he'd be waiting at the door.

He hadn't been, and she'd walked into the foyer, felt her stomach twist. No more glossy marble tiles or flowered wallpaper. Instead, dark wood floors stretched into the hallway, the once too-bright walls painted cream. The photos of Amelia still lined the walls, though. Baby. Toddler. Preschooler. Gabe hadn't been lying when he'd said he'd kept all the pictures out. Everywhere she'd looked, she'd seen her niece's chubby face or her sister's smiling one.

Her heart ached with it, and she'd wanted to turn around and leave. If there wasn't so much riding on this meeting, if she wasn't so desperate for answers, she might have done just that.

"I'm fine," she responded by rote, but she didn't feel fine. She felt sick.

"You're pale." He touched her cheek. Just a light touch of his finger. Then it was gone.

"I'm tired."

"And?" he pressed, and she couldn't keep looking into his eyes and not telling the truth.

"It's hard. Seeing all those pictures again."

"I'm sorry you have to go through this."

"I'm sorry my sister had to go through what she had to. I'm sorry for my niece. Whatever happened to her, she must have been terrified."

She swallowed down a hard knot of grief. "I want to know what happened. I want to know why. When they arrested Norman Meyers for the murders, it seemed like some random thing, as if my sister and niece were just in the wrong place at the wrong time. If Amelia is alive, that changes everything."

She walked to the mantel that had once been filled with bits and pieces of her sister's life. A pinecone she and Amelia had picked up at the park, spray painted with pink glitter and hung from their Christmas tree. A vase filled with a collection of flower petals that had fallen from every bouquet Gabe had given her. They were gone now, replaced by a simple framed photo of the family in happier times—Gabe, Lydia and Amelia.

"They were beautiful," he said quietly, and she turned to face him again, saw the compassion in his eyes and felt the ice around her heart melt a little.

"They were. Lydia had a lot of problems. I'm not going to lie. She did. She deserved better, though."

He nodded. Just that. No flowery words. No talk about how God had a plan for everything. She'd heard all that before. After Lydia's body was discovered, Harper had been surrounded by well-meaning people who'd all wanted to reassure her things would be okay.

But they couldn't be okay when the sister and niece she loved were gone.

"Ever since I got that package in the mail, I've been thinking about our last night, about all the things I wish I'd said."

"What do you wish you'd said?" he asked.

She could think of a dozen things—*I love you. You've always been my best friend. I'm so glad we're family.* Those were at the top of her list.

She didn't give voice to them, though. She couldn't. Not without her voice breaking and her heart shattering with it. "It doesn't matter. Lydia is gone. The opportunity to say what needed saying is gone, too."

"It matters." He lifted a small bowl from a side table, and she knew it was one of hers. The earthen tones, the subtle variations of colors. It was an earlier piece, the shape heavier and more solid than her newer pieces were, but it was definitely one of hers.

"Yours," Logan said, and then he turned it over, revealing her pseudonym. "Do you think he knows it?"

"I don't know." She took the bowl from his hand, turned it over. Her signature was etched into the bottom, those names so similar to ones

Gabe was familiar with that she doubted he hadn't known. "He might. The names would certainly be familiar to him."

"Interesting."

"What?"

"He didn't mention that you were a potter when I met with him before taking his case."

"Maybe he didn't think it was important." She shrugged. "Maybe he didn't really know."

"Seems like too much of a coincidence to me, Harper. Look at his house. This kind of art doesn't seem like something he'd buy."

True. Gabe had modern taste—clean lines, sharp angles, everything streamlined and neat.

"Even if he knew it was mine, he wouldn't have known where to find me. My agent doesn't even know my address."

"Maybe not, but I don't like being taken for a ride, and that's what this whole thing feels like—lies designed to get your brother-in-law what he wants." He took the bowl back and set it down.

"What, exactly, do you think he wants?"

"That's something we need to ask him." He lifted a framed photo that had been sitting beside the bowl. Gabe was in it. His hair just a little longer than it had been when she'd known him, his arm around a pretty brunette.

Maggie Johnson. His best friend when he was

in high school and college. Daughter of Senator Eric Johnson, she was a pediatric neurologist who was known for her charitable contributions and her compassion.

She was soft-spoken, calm, not easily rattled. The antithesis of Harper's sister, and maybe a better match for Gabe.

"His fiancée," Logan said.

"He mentioned that on the phone. They've been friends for a long time."

"Does it bother you that they're more than friends now?"

"It bothered me that they might have been more than friends before. Now? Lydia has been gone for four years. It's not hurting her."

That was only part of the truth.

The fact was, if she thought about it enough, she could be resentful that he'd moved on, found happiness, was living a life without Lydia in it.

She wouldn't think about it, though. She'd spent a year being bitter and angry. With God. With Lydia and Amelia's murderer. With Gabe. With herself. She'd spent that year rehashing her last moments with her sister and niece, blaming everyone and everything for failing to save them. At the end of that year, she'd sat down at an old potter's wheel that she'd bought secondhand, and she'd thrown her first bowl. It had been misshapen and rough, but she'd found solace in the work. In that solace, she'd found a little bit of peace.

"I didn't ask if it was hurting her, Harper," Logan said gently. "I asked if it bothered you. Now. Today. He was with this woman the night your sister and niece disappeared. It seems that might be a tough thing to swallow—that he's come full circle, ended up with the person who broke your sister's family apart."

"Maggie didn't break them apart. She was a bone of contention between Gabe and Lydia. I know that. My sister brought her up a lot, complained that she was too big a part of Gabe's life, but Gabe swore up and down they weren't having an affair. The night Lydia disappeared, she and Amelia were staying at my place. I guess Lydia and Gabe had had another one of their fights, and she'd told him she was coming to live with me."

"Had that happened before?"

"Once or twice. She'd come, stay the night and go back home. Lydia had it good with Gabe, and she knew it. I don't think there was anything that could have made her give that up."

"Not even Maggie?"

"Not even her. From what Gabe told the police, Maggie had lost a patient, and she'd stopped by Gabe's place because she was devastated. They'd talked until three in the morning, and then she went home. Maggie confirmed the story."

"You believed them?"

"Logan." She sighed, because she didn't want to talk about things that couldn't be changed. She wanted to see Gabe, find out what else he knew about the blond-haired girl who looked so much like Lydia. "I don't know what I believed. I was terrified. My sister was missing. My niece was missing. I had no idea where they'd gone. Three days later, Lydia's body was found, and everything just… It's a blur. I remember that Gabe's housekeeper confirmed the story. She let Maggie into the house around ten and served coffee and snacks. She didn't go to bed until Maggie left."

"A foolproof alibi for your brother-in-law, huh?"

"Yes."

"One that money could have bought?"

"It's not something I didn't think about at the time."

"But?"

"I was more worried about proving myself innocent than proving him guilty. Then Lydia's engagement ring was pawned and the police had another suspect, one who had Lydia's purse, her jewelry." She shrugged. "It seemed like the police had the killer."

"Did you think they did?"

"Most of the time. Other times, I wondered why my sister had left my house in the middle of the night, why she'd brought my niece. I wondered—"

Footsteps sounded in the hall, and she pressed her lips together, locking in the words and the accusation that she really had no business making. Gabe had been having affairs. That was what the press said. He might very well have wanted to get his lower-class wife out of the picture so he could hook up with someone a little more on his level. That was what people whispered behind his back. She didn't know if any of it was true. She knew that was what Lydia had worried about. She knew her sister had been afraid of losing Gabe. She didn't know if there was justification for that.

A tiny gray-haired woman stepped into the room, her starched white blouse and crisp black slacks belying the lateness of the hour. Adeline had been working for the Wilsons longer than Gabe had been alive. She'd been there before he'd married Lydia. She was as much of a fixture in the house as any of the light switches or wall sconces, and she wasn't afraid to make her opinion about things known. Based on the scowl she'd been wearing when she'd opened the door to let Harper and Logan in, she wasn't happy with their early-morning visit.

"Mr. Wilson insists that I offer you coffee or tea while you're waiting," she nearly spat. "Would you like any?"

"I'm fine," Harper responded. Water would have been nice, but there was no way she was going to ask for some.

"You, sir?" Adeline asked, spearing Logan with a look that would have felled lesser men. He didn't seem intimidated by it. Maybe because he towered over her by at least a foot.

"No, thank you. My friends might. They're waiting in the SUV."

"One of them is. The other one is walking your dog through the back gardens." She tilted her chin, her eyes blazing black fire. "Those gardens cost a small fortune to maintain."

"I'd be happy to tell them to keep the dog in the front yard," Logan responded easily.

"No need. Mr. Wilson said it's fine. Otherwise, I'd have told them myself. Since he insists that we be polite to people who were rude enough to drag us out of bed in the wee hours of the morning, I'll go out and see if your friends want something."

"Before you do," Logan said, "can you give us some idea of when Mr. Wilson is going to make an appearance?"

"He's trying to locate the files that contain the information you're here for. He called his assistant to get some help with it. She should be here shortly. As for Mr. Wilson, he'll make an appearance when he's good and ready," Adeline snapped, turning on her heel and marching out of the room. Seconds later, the front door opened and slammed shut.

"Wow," Logan murmured. "She's something else."

"She worked for Gabe's dad for three decades. He and his wife moved to Florida ten years ago, and they didn't take her with them."

"I wonder why?"

"My sister said the same thing. When her in-laws moved, they deeded the house to Gabe. Adeline came with it. She's the gift that keeps on giving. That's what Lydia always said."

"I think I would have refused the gift," Logan said, the comment prompting a laugh out of Harper.

"Thanks," she said. "I needed that."

"Yeah. You did. You were looking a little overwhelmed."

"I am a little overwhelmed," she responded.

She shouldn't have been glad he was there, but she was. Having him around made her feel less alone, and she needed that more than she needed jokes and laughter.

"It's got to be strange coming back here after so many years."

"Strange is one way to put it."

"What's another?" He sat on the couch, pulling her down beside her. They were close enough that she could feel the heat of his thigh through her jeans, the warmth of his arm as she leaned back.

"Sad. Lydia loved this place so much."

"She didn't love Adeline."

"True. She didn't, but that was mostly because Adeline didn't like her."

"Was there a reason for that?" he asked, his arm stretched along the back of the sofa, his forearm so close to her head, she could have leaned back just a little and rested against it.

"My sister barely graduated from high school. She didn't go to college. She and Gabe met while she was waiting tables at a local restaurant."

"So she wasn't high class enough for Adeline?"

"That was what Lydia thought. Of course, Lydia had a lot of hang-ups, so she could have been misreading Adeline."

"You lived here for a year, right?"

"Yes," she responded, surprised that he knew the information. She doubted there were many people who remembered that. "Lydia was terrified that she wouldn't be a good enough mother. She asked me to move in and help out, and I agreed. I was in my last year of college, and I figured it would be cheaper to stay with her than to stay on campus another year."

"So you had a good opportunity to see how Adeline and Lydia interacted," he commented, and she nodded. She'd had a good opportunity to see how the entire family interacted, and she hadn't been impressed. She'd told herself a thousand times that things would be different when she married Daniel, that the two of them would have better communication, a more in-sync relationship.

They'd never gotten married, so her mental list of how she wanted things had amounted to a whole lot of dreams and nothing more.

Still, she could remember the tension in Gabe's home, the arguments she'd heard through closed doors while she'd rocked Amelia to sleep. Arguments about finances, about women, about the baby. Adeline hadn't been involved in any of them, but she'd listened. Harper had caught her a couple of times, hovering just on the other side of the office door or just outside the master bedroom.

"Adeline and Lydia didn't communicate much," she said, pushing aside the memories. "I think Adeline thought she was a little above Lydia, and Lydia had no patience for people. She was concerned about herself, her husband and her baby. That was about it. It wasn't the best of situations for either of them."

"But they both stuck it out."

"They both loved Gabe."

"Adeline is the housekeeper. *Love* seems like a strong word."

"She basically raised him, Logan. His mother had some mental health issues. Depression or bipolar. I don't know if they ever put a name to it. I don't think that's what kept her from being a good parent, but from what I understand, she was absent more than she was present when he was a kid." She'd heard bits and pieces of the story while she was living in the house, but she hadn't been all that interested. She'd been more concerned with making it through her last year of college, trying to salvage her relationship with Daniel, doing all the things that a college student did—all of it while helping Lydia.

"Thinking about it bothers you," he said, lifting her hand, pressing her fingers open. She hadn't realized she'd been clenching her fists, but she'd managed to gouge crescents into her palm, her short nails digging deep welts into the skin.

He smoothed his finger over the marks, his skin rough and warm. Her pulse jumped with feelings she didn't want to have—warmth, attraction, the feeling that this guy had something special to offer, something only he would ever be able to give.

Had she felt that way with Daniel?

She couldn't remember. She should probably be able to. If the relationship had been as important as she'd thought it was, if he'd been the guy she'd built him up to be, shouldn't she remember the way his fingers had felt on her arm, the way his arms had felt when they wrapped her in a hug?

All she could remember was the last time she'd seen him—not a bit of guilt in his eyes as he'd told her that he'd found someone else.

"Lots of things bother me, Logan." She tugged her hand from his and stood, pacing back to the door that led into the hall. "Like waiting for Gabe when I know that he was awake before we even got to the front door."

"A power game," he said simply, beside her again, just a few inches away, his jacket open, his shoulder holster visible beneath it.

"I don't like games."

"Then, we have something in common." He smiled, stepping out into the hall and heading to the staircase.

"Where are you going?" she whispered, hurrying after him, because she didn't want to stand in the hallway, looking at dozens of photos of her sister and niece.

"To find him."

"You can't just barge upstairs."

"Watch me." He was already on the third step, heading up the wide curved stairway, and she was right behind him. She knew the way to the master suite, knew where the nursery was—or had been. Had Gabe changed it?

They were on the landing when the front door opened and Adeline hustled inside, a petite dark-haired woman beside her. Black hair cut short, the hairstyle sleek and trendy. Large blue eyes. Full lips that might have had some help from collagen. Thin brows and thick lashes. Pretty. Professional in dark slacks and a simple cardigan set nearly covered by a black wool coat. She looked familiar, and Harper tried to put the face with a name, but the memory was just out of reach.

The woman knew her, though.

Her eyes widened, and she smiled, rushing forward to pull Harper in for a hug. "Harper! It's been forever. When Gabe said you were here, I almost couldn't believe it. But—" she stepped back, the smile still in place "—here you are."

"Yes. I wanted some information about—"

"Amelia. That whole mess with someone sending that picture." The woman shook her head, her hair barely moving, and something about the way she cocked her head to the side sparked another just-out-of-reach memory. "We've got copies of everything on file in Gabe's office here, but he's not sure where it is. He said I could just tell him, but this will be easier. I can find it myself in two seconds flat. How about we go in the office and wait for him?"

Easier how?

That was what Logan wanted to know. The woman had left home in the middle of the night to drive to her boss's house to help him find a file? Seemed strange to him, but when she turned her overly made-up eyes on him, he just smiled.

"Logan Fitzgerald," he said, offering his hand.

She clasped it briefly, nodded. "Sandra Williams. Gabe's secretary/assistant/right-hand man. We spoke on the phone when I set up your meetings with him."

"Right." He remembered. The woman had been very efficient and very specific. She'd called with a date for their first meeting, a time, a place—not at the office because Gabe hadn't wanted to draw attention to what he was doing. She'd been matter-of-fact without being too abrupt, but he'd had the feeling she'd felt as if calling him was a waste of her valuable time.

"Sandra?" Harper exclaimed, her eyes wide with shock. "Sandra Williams from Suitland High School?"

"You didn't recognize me?" Sandra laughed, but Logan didn't see a whole lot of good humor in her eyes. "I guess I've changed a little in the past few years."

"It has been a while," Harper murmured. She still looked surprised and uneasy.

"Five years. I was so sorry that I couldn't come back for Lydia's…" Her voice trailed off, and she blinked tears from her eyes. "Her funeral. And Amelia's." She cleared her throat. "I had some major clients in New York who I was working for, and I couldn't get away."

"I understand," Harper responded, reaching out to touch Sandra's arm.

"I don't. I've never been able to forgive myself. Lydia and I were best friends until I moved away, and then…" She shook her head. "I wish I'd never gone to New York. The time I spent there was such a waste, but I guess I had to try, and Lydia supported me a hundred percent in going for my dreams."

Harper nodded. "I remember her telling me about your move."

"Did she?"

"Yes. She was excited for you. Of course, she was about to get married, and she was distracted. Otherwise she'd have made the trip to New York and helped you move."

"That's the kind of person she was," Sandra said with a sigh. "The office is this way." She led the way down the hall, bypassing the sitting room where Logan and Harper had been waiting. The house was immense by Logan's standards, probably close to ten thousand square feet. The hallway was long, wide and lined with framed photos that Harper seemed to be studiously avoiding looking at.

Sandra turned left into another wing of the house. Just a short hallway and double doors.

She fished a key from her pocket, unlocked the doors and opened them. "Come on in. I'm sure Gabe won't mind. He's generally very hospitable."

"Not when I've been woken at two in the morning," Gabe said as he rounded the corner behind them.

He didn't look like a guy who'd been woken. He looked wide-awake, his dark slacks and white button-down shirt wrinkle-free, his black shoes polished to a high sheen. Hair cut short, eyes sharp. He met Logan's gaze, then shifted his attention to Harper.

"It's been a while, Harper."

"Yes." She didn't move toward him, and he didn't offer a hand or a hug. They both seemed tense, whatever thoughts or words they needed to say hidden behind a veil of civility.

Logan would have to break through that.

He wanted the truth. All of it. Without that, he wasn't going to be able to keep Harper safe.

"I'd say that I've missed you, but my life has been pretty hectic the past few years, and I haven't really had time to miss anyone." He walked into the office, Sandra so close to his side they could have been one person.

"You've missed Lydia and Amelia," Sandra corrected him, and he frowned.

"I'm sure that Harper understood that," he said.

Harper didn't comment. She'd moved across the room, her shoulders slumped, her face pale. French doors looked out onto a dark yard, and she stopped there, visible to anyone who might be looking, backlit by the office.

Not a place he wanted her to be.

He stepped between her and the glass. "How about we not stand in front of glass doors?"

"How about we get the answers we came for?" she responded, and he nodded, because he understood the feeling of wanting to know, of being desperate for answers, for proof, for something that justified hope.

"Okay," he said, nudging her back. "But not while we're standing in front of the doors."

"I'll get that file," Sandra said cheerfully, her bright voice at odds with the situation. Maybe that was the way she reacted to stress, but Logan thought it was odd. He thought the entire household was odd—Gabe, Adeline, the ten thousand or so square feet of space that two people lived in. Odd didn't mean criminal, though. Then again, it didn't mean innocent.

Gabe had plenty of money and plenty of power. He could afford to hire people to keep his lawn looking perfect, to wash his windows and paint his house. He could afford fancy suits and huge offices, and Logan had no doubt he could afford to hire people to do his dirty work.

Had he?

That was the question Logan wanted an answer to.

It was just a matter of time before he got it. Nothing could stay secret forever; nothing could remain hidden. The truth would come out, and whoever was after Harper would be stopped.

Logan just hoped that Harper wouldn't be hurt in the process.

NINE

Harper wasn't sure what she was hoping to see when Sandra took a folder from the cabinet and handed it to Gabe. Definitive evidence that proved Amelia was alive? Some hint at the truth?

Her pulse pounded at the thought, her muscles tightening with the need to do something. If Amelia was alive, she had to have some memories of her mother, her father, her family, friends and school. Had she wondered why no one had come for her? Had she cried for the people she loved?

The thought was heartbreaking, and Harper tried to push it away as Gabe opened the folder and took out several sheaves of paper.

"This is it. Not much. Just the photo and picture of the piece of blanket I was sent. The police took it as evidence earlier this evening." He handed the papers to her. "There's also the police report from four years ago, and a report from a private detective I hired after I got the package. He wasn't able to discover anything more than what the police have."

"Which is?" Logan asked as he reached for the papers.

"The package was mailed from a post office in Silver Spring. The employees don't have any memory of the person who sent it, but security footage collected by the police captured the guy paying cash to mail it."

"Have the police identified the person?"

"No. Although they called me this evening and said they might have a lead. They stopped by and took the piece of blanket, said they're running some tests on it, looking for DNA. I'm going down to the station in the morning to meet with Detective Willard. You remember him, Harper?"

"He would be difficult to forget," she murmured, her gaze focused on the picture Logan had handed her. She'd seen the resemblance between her sister and the girl in the texted photo. The resemblance was even more obvious in the larger version of the picture. The green of the eyes, the tiny dimple in the cheek, the shape of the chin… They were so much like Lydia's, Harper's breath caught, her heart skipping a beat and then another.

"Breathe," Logan whispered in her ear. She

sucked in a deep breath and dropped into a chair near the desk.

"This could be a photo of Lydia when she was this age," she managed to say, her voice thick with tears.

She wasn't going to cry, though.

She'd wept buckets of tears after Lydia's body was discovered, a bucket more after police had closed the missing-persons case on Amelia and said she'd most likely died with her mother.

She'd cried, and it had done her no good.

Now she felt hollow eyed and tired.

"I thought the same," Gabe said quietly, his voice rough edged and gruff. "I have all those old photos from when you two were kids. I took them out after I got this, because I didn't want to think..." He shook his head.

"That she was alive?" Harper finished, because that was how she felt. "And we gave up on her?"

There. It was out. The words hanging in the air, ugly and horrible and so true they'd had to be said.

"Yes." Just that one word, but there was a world of brokenness and hurt in it, four years of struggles and pain.

All the anger Harper had, all the suspicion, all the feelings that somehow Gabe was to blame seeped away.

"There was nothing you could have done, Gabe," Sandra said, touching his arm, her nails long and painted deep red. They seemed out of place right then. Garish. She couldn't have known she'd be pulled out of bed before dawn, brought into a situation that would open old wounds, but still...

Those nails.

Harper looked away—she didn't want to see the glossy nails, the sympathetic expression that seemed almost overdrawn in the quiet that had descended.

"You've gotten the FBI involved, right? What are they saying?" Logan asked, breaking the silence and refocusing the conversation. Away from the guilt. Toward something productive.

Gabe nodded, stepping away from Sandra's hand. "Detective Willard contacted them. They've run facial-recognition software, comparing the photo I received to old photos of Amelia and Lydia."

"And?" Logan prodded.

"And they think there's a good chance the girl in that picture is my daughter."

"What?" Harper jumped up, nearly tipping over the chair as she swung around to face him. "You didn't tell me that!"

"I didn't know until after we spoke." He shrugged as if it didn't matter, but they both knew it did. "I knew you were already on the way. I figured it was the kind of news that should be given in person."

"Maybe you should have given it a little faster," she snapped. "I've been here for—"

"Let's not go after each other. We have bigger fish to fry," Logan said, his hands settling on her shoulders, his thumbs brushing against her neck. She shivered and almost stepped back into his arms, let herself get a little closer to his warmth.

"Like whoever took my daughter," Gabe spat, his eyes flashing with anger. "And the police who screwed up so much that they thought she was dead. I've missed four years of her life. Four years!"

"*If* she's alive," Sandra broke in, her perfectly lined and mascaraed eyes darting from Gabe to Harper. "He's absolutely convinced she is, but facial-recognition software—"

"Is pretty accurate." Gabe raked a hand through his hair. "She's alive. I'm going to find her."

"How do you plan to do that?" Logan asked, his hands still cupping Harper's shoulders.

She could have stepped away, but she didn't.

For the first time in more years than she could remember, she wanted support. Needed it, because her legs felt shaky, her stomach twisting with a terrible mix of hope and fear.

"Tomorrow morning, national news stations are running stories on Amelia's disappearance. The police and FBI arranged it. Someone, somewhere has seen that little girl." He jabbed his thumb toward the photo. "Someone knows who she is, and I'm praying that whoever it is comes forward. If they don't…it won't matter. I'm hiring another private detective. I'm combing this entire country, putting all my resources into finding out where she is."

"You've got a wedding to plan," Sandra pointed out, and Gabe shot her a look that was so dark and hard, she took a step back.

"Do you really think I care about a wedding when my daughter may be alive?"

"I think—" Sandra began, but footsteps in the hall cut off the words. Not the soft pad of Adeline's rubber-soled shoes. This sounded like the clack of heels on tile.

Seconds later, a tall, dark-haired woman appeared at the office door. Green scrubs. Hair pulled back from a pale face. Maggie Johnson looked as if she'd just finished a long shift at the hospital. Somehow, she still managed to look pleasant, her soft prettiness something that Lydia had often mocked.

Harper had never had a problem with it or

with the woman. Maggie had always been pleasant and kind to her, to Lydia and to Amelia. As far as Harper had seen, there'd been no jealousy, no hint of wanting what someone else had, nothing that would have indicated she was having an affair with Gabe.

Yet now, four years after Lydia's death, the two were a couple.

Did it mean anything?

Harper didn't know, didn't think she was objective enough to figure it out, because losing Lydia still hurt. Losing Amelia...

She lifted the photo of the girl, her heart pounding, then eyed the photo of the piece of blanket. It looked exactly like the one she'd received.

Maybe they hadn't lost Amelia. Not for good anyway.

"Maggie!" Gabe said, rushing forward to take his fiancée into his arms. They looked good together, both tall, lean and attractive.

Harper didn't want to notice, but she did.

She also didn't want to be standing there, watching the kiss the two exchanged. She'd told Logan that the relationship didn't bother her. It hadn't. Until now. Until she was face-to-face with it, looking at the man who'd once passionately kissed her sister sweetly kissing someone else.

There was a lot of love in that kiss. A lot of tenderness. A lot of things she'd never seen between Gabe and Lydia, and maybe it *did* hurt. Maybe it did make her a little angry, a little sad, a little melancholy.

She turned blindly, nearly walking into Logan's chest.

"Careful," he said.

"Sorry," she murmured, stepping past him and running from the office.

He was following. She could hear his footsteps on the tile, but he didn't say anything as she rushed through the hallway filled with memories and ran to the front door. She jerked it open, lunged out into the cold, crisp November morning, took deep, shaky breaths of air.

It didn't help.

Nothing could.

Not the predawn silence. Not the Christmas lights sparkling on trees that lined Gabe's driveway. Not the moon dipping low in the sky, or the soft call of a mourning dove.

Lydia was dead. Gabe had moved on.

And somewhere out in the big, wide world, Amelia might be alive, living with strangers.

Not strangers anymore, her mind whispered, and that was awful, too. What if the girl in the picture had moved on the way Gabe had? What if she really was Amelia, but she'd forgotten the mother who'd raised her for four years? The father who'd adored her? The aunt who'd made her chocolate-chip pancakes on snowy winter mornings?

What if she had a new family she loved? People who loved her?

Would that be better than the alternative—Amelia being abused and mistreated? Amelia missing her mother, her father, her aunt, her friends?

"Time to go," Logan said, his arm suddenly around her waist, his words ruffling the fine hair near her ear.

"I still need to—"

"You can do it tomorrow."

"But—"

"It's time to go, Harper," he said again. "Because there's nothing you can do here that can't be done at the safe house."

"There's nothing I can do at the safe house that I can't do here. Except talk to Gabe and work on figuring this out."

"He's talking to his fiancée." He moved down the porch stairs, and she was moving with him. The truth was, she didn't want to be in the house with Gabe and Maggie.

"Eventually he won't be."

"Eventually the sun will come up," he responded. "Eventually a new day will begin.

Eventually the news stories about your niece will air, and someone somewhere will see them."

"And call the police?" They'd reached the SUV, and Harper didn't have the energy to argue about where they were going or what they would do.

The fact was, Logan was right.

There was nothing she could do at Gabe's place.

Not now.

Tomorrow, though, after the story aired, she wanted to talk to him more, talk to Detective Willard, the FBI, the post office employee who'd accepted the package with the photo in it.

"I'm praying that's what happens," Logan said as he opened the back door and gestured for her to get in.

Malone was already there, sitting against the far door, the kitten in his lap.

He met her eyes and gave her a brief nod.

"Where's Stella?" Logan asked as he climbed in beside Harper.

"Walking the dog."

"She's been doing that for a while," Logan said, reaching for the door handle. "Maybe I'd better go check on her."

"Don't think that will be necessary." Malone gestured to a dark shadow moving around the side of the house. "Looks as if she's back. Good thing. I'm beat, and sitting here doing nothing isn't making me any more energetic."

"Would you rather there be some action?" Logan asked, and Malone shrugged.

"I'd rather be sleeping, but since I can't have that, I'd rather be driving somewhere I can sleep."

"Have you heard from Chance?" Logan asked as Stella opened the back for Picasso. The big dog scrambled in, shoving his head over the seat to nuzzle Harper's hair.

"Did you miss me?" she asked, rubbing his muzzle as Stella hopped into the driver's seat.

Picasso whined in response, his tail thumping rhythmically.

"He missed you," Stella grumbled. "I missed you. We all missed you, because we all want to get to the safe house, get some food in our bellies and get to sleep."

"I didn't mean to hold things up. My brother-in-law took his sweet time making an appearance."

"Bet he's usually like that, isn't he?" Stella asked, backing down the long driveway, her short hair brushing her nape as she glanced over her shoulder.

"Like what?" Harper asked.

"Like making people wait for him but not

being all that patient about having to wait. Like wanting other people to be more conscious of his time than he is of theirs."

"That's how my sister described him," she responded. Lydia had complained that Gabe was a hard taskmaster, that he wanted things done a certain way and wasn't happy if they weren't. She'd complained about Gabe making her late and about him forcing her to be early. No rhyme or reason. Just his timing or he didn't participate.

But Lydia had complained about a lot of things, and Harper had learned to listen with half an ear, not always giving her full attention to whatever the day's gripe was about.

"How would you describe him?" Malone asked.

"Probably the same way. He likes to be in control, and he likes to be the one to call the shots."

"I like to eat. At regular times. I also like to not have to walk an oversize dog through someone's flower beds," Stella muttered.

There was nothing to say to that, so Harper kept her mouth shut.

Up ahead, the wrought iron gates that separated the community from the world beyond stood closed, huge Christmas wreaths hanging from brick posts beside them. The fence that surrounded the neighborhood had been hung with garlands and decorated with white lights, the entire display elegantly festive.

Christmas was just around the corner.

How would the little girl with blond hair be spending it?

With a family that loved her?

With memories of Christmases past?

With haunting nightmares of a mother who'd been murdered?

Harper shuddered, and Logan pulled off his coat and wrapped it around her shoulders. It smelled like masculinity and strength, felt like the warmth of home. She burrowed in deeper, trying desperately not to think about Amelia and all the years that might have been lost.

"You okay?" Logan asked, and she nodded, because the truth was too complicated to speak.

She was okay and she wasn't, and that was a difficult thing to explain. An impossible one.

For as long as she could remember, she'd known that God had a plan. That He'd work things out. That no matter what, everything would be okay.

Her mother hadn't been much of a parent, but she'd brought her girls to church and taught them to thank God for their blessings, go to God with their burdens.

It had taken a long time for those old habits

to become outpourings of faith. Harper didn't think they had until after her sister's murder. In the past few years, though, she had relied more on her faith and less on herself.

No more striving for success. No more frantic scrambling to get ahead. Now she prayed and waited and tried to trust that God's will would be done.

Tried.

But, right now, all the old disappointments flooded her mind, all the times that she'd prayed and not gotten what she'd hoped for lingered there.

She wanted to scramble and work and try and fight. She wanted to do everything in her power to learn the truth.

She wanted, more than anything, to bring Amelia home.

If Amelia was alive.

If.

The gates swung open, and Stella navigated the SUV through, pulling onto a main thoroughfare that led to the Beltway.

Harper had been down this street dozens of times. Nothing had changed. The lawns of outlying properties were still immaculately kept. Mature trees still lined both sides of the road.

To the left, a large church jutted up against the night sky, the churchyard filled with old tombstones. The cemetery had closed years ago, but the church remained open. Gabe and Lydia had gotten married there, had attended services there every Sunday.

The memories were right at the back of Harper's mind—the wedding, Amelia's birth, her first Christmas, the sweet blue velvet dress Lydia had put her in, the shiny black patent leather shoes that had fallen off her feet.

Harper was so caught up in the memories, so filled with what had been, that she almost missed Malone's subtle movement, his shift from relaxation to tension.

Almost, but she felt the shift, heard Picasso whine softly.

The hair on the back of her neck stood on end, and she glanced at Logan, saw that he was staring out the side window, his gaze focused on the cemetery.

Did he see something?

She wanted to ask but was afraid of distracting him.

Whatever was going on, Stella must have sensed it, too. She stepped on the gas, the SUV shooting forward.

"Get down," Logan barked, and she was suddenly leaning forward with someone pressed against her back.

Glass shattered. Picasso howled.

Logan shouted something, but she couldn't hear the words past the pulsing of blood in her ears.

Another shout. More glass shattering.

An explosion of gunfire, and the SUV swerved, spun, wheels shrieking as more gunshots filled the air.

The SUV came to a jarring halt, and Malone opened his door, cold air seeping into the SUV as he ran, Picasso scrambling over the seat and following him.

Sirens screamed, the kitten howled and Stella spoke calmly. Probably into her phone. Harper couldn't see anything except her knees and the floor. Harper tried to nudge Logan away so she could breathe and see and *think*.

"Stay down!" he growled.

She didn't have much of a choice, and she didn't have enough air in her lungs to tell him that.

Seconds later, he shifted, his weight gone, breath filling Harper's lungs.

"Do. Not. Move," he commanded, and then he was gone, the door slamming closed, the sirens still screaming.

She waited. A heartbeat. Two.

Then she eased up, her heart hammering in her chest, her body shaking with adrenaline.

Cold air wafted in from the shattered front

window, a few branches of a big tree brushing against the vehicle's hood.

Harper eased up a little more, trying to see into the front seat. Stella was there, gun in hand, eyes trained on the darkness beyond the window.

"He said not to move," Stella muttered, her voice thick and a little slurred.

"What happened?"

"Ambush. At least two shooters. One on either side of the road." She swiped blood from a cut on her cheek, but her gaze never wavered.

"Were you hit?" Harper climbed into the front seat, ignoring Stella's muttered warning and using Logan's jacket to wipe at the seeping wound. "This is pretty deep."

"It's just from glass. I'll be fine."

"You need stitches."

"What I need," Stella responded, "is for you to do what Logan said. Stay down. These guys aren't shooting at us, Harper. They're after you."

True, but there was no way Harper was going to cower behind a seat while other people fought her battles for her.

She dabbed at the wound again, and Stella brushed her hand away.

"Enough. I'll deal with that after the police arrive."

"They're here," Harper said. The lights of

the approaching squad cars flashed in the rear-view mirror.

"Good. Stay here. I'll talk to them."

She was out of the car before Harper could reply.

The yowling kitten hopped into Harper's lap, and she could have sat where she was, waiting for the problem to be dealt with.

Could have, but wasn't going to.

She'd spent most of her life taking care of herself. She wasn't going to stop now.

She set the kitten on the seat and hopped out of the SUV, cold, crisp air enveloping her as she moved toward the police cars.

Two shooters. Double the trouble. Double the chance of getting killed. Except one of them was dead, shot by Malone, his body lying beside the road.

Logan didn't have any intention of letting the other gunman take him down. He had a score to settle.

He'd been set up, used as a pawn to get Harper. He wasn't sure why, had no idea how all the pieces of the puzzle fit together, but he was going to find out.

Fifty yards away, Malone moved through the cemetery, his dark figure nearly blending with the deeper shadows of the grave sites and monuments. Picasso moved beside him, surprisingly silent and focused, his nose to the ground, his tail stiff.

He'd scented something.

The perp?

That would be convenient.

It would be easy.

It could be dangerous.

The puppy had no idea what he was doing. He wasn't a trained police dog, and if he got in the way, he could get shot. Or get someone else shot.

Something to think of for the next time.

For now, they had to keep moving forward.

He signaled, indicating that he was heading toward the church, and Malone signaled back. He'd take the east side of the building. Eventually they'd meet up. Hopefully they'd have the perp cornered.

Logan headed west, aiming for the back corner of the old stone building. Its steeple reached toward the sky, the hulking tower gothic and old. He'd never been in this area of town, had no reason to hang out in some of the more posh areas of DC. His place was in a middle-class area, where urban sprawl had settled into a nice, tight-knit neighborhood.

Even there, crime happened, danger lurked.

If there was one thing Logan had learned

during his time in the military, it was to expect trouble.

He was expecting it now, his gun in hand, his breathing soft and controlled. He forced it to be that way, not wanting to mask the sound of a quiet approach.

He reached the building, skirted around the side and made his way along the edge. Nothing. Not a footprint stamped into the dry grass.

He had that feeling, though. The one that said trouble was nearby. It niggled at the back of his mind. He scanned the area, eying the grassy slope that stretched from the building to a narrow copse of trees.

He could see lights and houses through them. A car zipping past.

Civilization and civility, but a monster hid in the shadows. He sensed him like he sensed the dawn hovering just beneath the horizon.

Voices carried on the quiet air, distant but drawing near. The police, probably. Maybe with their own K-9 team. A man had been shot dead. A woman was wounded. Not badly. Stella had insisted she was fine, had told him if he didn't get out of the SUV and go after the perp, she'd do it herself.

He'd gone, because she would have done it if he'd been the one with the bleeding gash on his face.

First rule of engagement—secure the scene.

Until it was secured, no one was safe.

He stopped at the corner of the building, looking out into an empty parking lot. Across it, a shed sat sheltered by tall pines and an old oak. The darkness was thick there, the shadows impenetrable. If Logan were looking for a place to hide, that was where he'd have headed. A good vantage point to see both corners of the building, a good place to stage an ambush.

He'd wait the perp out, see if he showed himself.

That was another thing he'd learned in the military—patience. Rushing in could get a guy killed, and Logan had no desire to die. He had Christmas to attend with siblings he hadn't seen in too long.

The job.

Always getting in the way of his personal life.

That was fine.

It was good.

Sometimes, though, it was lonely.

This year, he wouldn't spend Christmas in a foreign country. This year, he'd be home on the farm, where he'd spent his growing-up years. Where his parents had built something solid and nice, something Logan's brother was maintaining. He'd bring a bagful of gifts and he'd eat boatloads of food, and when it was over, he'd go home, and he'd thank God that he'd had the opportunity.

Yeah. He had to stay alive.

And that meant playing it smart.

He stuck to the shadowy edge of the building, the voices behind him drifting on the crisp air. The police would be there soon. If the perp were around, he'd need to make his move fast or he'd be trapped.

The cold metal of the gun pressed into his palm. The shivering chill of the air seeped through his shirt. He didn't move and didn't hear Malone or the dog moving, either.

Nothing. For a heartbeat. Two. Nothing for the time it took several cars to pass on a nearby road.

Nothing, and then a shadow seemed to undulate near the shed.

There!

It separated itself from the blackness, ducked beneath a pine bough and disappeared.

TEN

Logan moved across the parking lot and eased into the trees where the perp had been hiding. The shed was small, the door locked. The guy had probably been hoping to find a way inside, maybe bunk down there until he lost his tail. There were no windows, though. No way to break in except the door.

Logan walked past the shed and through the trees, stepping out into a wide field.

He scanned the area, heard something coming through the trees behind him.

Some*one*.

Not Malone. He'd have signaled, and he'd have been a lot quieter about it. Logan holstered his gun and ducked back into the shelter of the pine boughs, took position behind a thick-trunked tree and waited. Twigs snapped. Leaves crunched. A shadow appeared.

He didn't hesitate, didn't give the guy time to realize he'd been seen. He threw himself at the figure, knocking the guy off his feet before he had a chance to realize what was happening.

It took about two seconds to disarm the guy, a little longer to get him to give up the fight.

By the time he did, Malone was there, Picasso growling at his side.

"Took you long enough," Logan said, dragging the perp to his feet.

The guy was young, about six foot, lean, his face pockmarked from drug use. He looked more dazed than dangerous.

"Hey," he said, yanking against Logan's hold. "Let me go!"

"So you can shoot at us again?" Malone asked, and the perp struggled harder.

"I didn't shoot at anyone. I was minding my own business—"

"Tell you what," Logan interrupted, because he wanted to get back to the SUV and check on Stella and on Harper. "How about you save it for the police?"

"Police? We don't need no police. Me and my friend was minding our own business, walking through the churchyard and some guy, he comes up to us and he says, 'You want to make some money?' And I said yeah, because who doesn't need money? And he says, 'We're just going to play a prank on my friends. Scare them a little, just fire a couple of shots at their car.' We weren't supposed to hurt anyone." The man was still talking as Logan dragged him back toward the church.

"You know your buddy is dead, right?" Logan asked, cutting the guy off, because he was tired and wasn't in the mood to listen to the lie.

"You killed Drake?" the kid asked, all the bravado gone from his face.

"He killed himself. Or as good as killed himself." Malone didn't sound all that sorry for the death. He sounded resigned. "You shoot at someone who has a gun, you've got to expect that they're going to shoot back."

"He didn't tell us you had guns," the perp said, then pressed his lips together as if he knew he'd said too much.

"Who didn't tell you?" Logan asked.

"The guy who asked us to…help him out."

"By scaring his friends?" Logan prodded, and the kid had the decency to keep his mouth shut. Maybe he realized the lie wasn't going to work, that with his friend dead, he had no one to back up his story. Maybe he was sorry he and his buddy had agreed to ambush the SUV. Probably he was sorry about that. His friend was dead. No amount of money was worth that.

"How much did you get paid?" Malone asked. "Was it the value of your friend's life?"

That was all it took, and the kid started blubbering, his eyes seeping, his nose running, his sobs echoing through the night.

They wouldn't get any more out of him. The police would have to do that.

They'd reached the church, and several police officers were moving toward them, flashlights dancing across the ground.

"Hold it right there," one called out. "Drop your weapons. Keep your hands where we can see them."

Logan did what he was told. No sense getting himself shot by the good guys. They'd sort things out. Eventually. In the meantime, the perp was in custody, and he had a story to tell. One that Logan was really anxious to hear.

"I'm putting the gun down," he said, making his intentions very clear as he lowered it to the pavement. Then he waited impatiently while the police slapped handcuffs on all three of them, frisked them and separated them for questioning. Logan stood silently while his credentials were checked, his story confirmed. Finally, his Glock was handed back and his wallet was returned.

"Good enough," the officer said. "We'll want to take an official statement, but your story matches what the ladies said—self-defense. Glad you were able to take the guy out before he took one of you out."

"Are the women still back at the SUV?" Logan asked.

"Ambulance took them away. One needs stitches. The other insisted on going with her."

That was not what Logan wanted to hear.

Sure, a hospital sounded safe. That was the problem. Assuming she was safe because she was surrounded by medical professionals, patients and visitors was a sure way for Harper to get into trouble.

"Did an officer go with them?"

"Someone is going to meet them there." The policeman didn't seem concerned. He was more focused on the notes he was writing than the words he was saying.

"They were almost killed, Officer. Your department didn't think it was necessary to give them an escort?"

That got the guy's attention. He looked up from his notepad and scowled. "My department has its hands full tonight, Fitzgerald. Two murders. Three robberies. Five shootings, and now the mess you people have brought with you." He waved toward the perp, who was sitting on the ground, police officers flanking him. The medical examiner's van that was parked near the SUV.

"We didn't bring him or his friend. They're local."

"You brought your troubles," the officer responded. "So here's the deal. A homicide detective is meeting the ladies at the hospital. Guy by the name of Thomas Willard. You know him?"

"Not personally."

"But you know of him, right?" he pressed, and Logan nodded. "That's what I thought. He's sticking his nose in this case for whatever reason, and I'm not going to tell him to get out of it. He called my supervisor, told him that he'd be at the hospital when the victims arrived. I'm assuming he's there. That's about all I can do. Like I said, I have my hands full."

"Understood," Logan said, keeping his voice neutral. He knew how difficult police work was, and he wasn't going to press the guy for more than what he could give.

"You want to head to the hospital, you're welcome to do it. I've got your contact information. I'll call if I need more from you."

"Will you call when you get more from him?" He nodded toward the perpetrator.

"Soon as I have five seconds to breathe," the officer said, fishing a card from his pocket and handing it to Logan. "Take this. You don't hear from me in a couple of days, give me a call."

"Thanks."

"It's my job," he said, but Logan was already walking away. He bypassed Malone, who was still being questioned. He didn't stop to chat.

They'd hook up later. For now, he had one goal—make sure Harper was safe.

Stella handled getting five stitches in her cheek a lot better than Harper handled seeing her get them.

Which was odd, because she'd never been squeamish about blood or needles. Right now, though, she felt light-headed and a little faint.

"If you pass out," Stella said as the emergency room doctor placed the last stitch, "I will take a photo of you lying on the floor and post it to social media."

"I'm not on social media, so it won't affect me one way or another," she replied, her mouth a little dry, her stomach churning.

"Okay. How about this? You pass out, and I'll tell them to leave you lying on the floor until Logan and Malone show up. I'll let one of them scrape you off the ground."

The thought of either of the men lifting her from the ground was enough to clear her head.

"I hope they're okay," she said.

"The men are fine. If they weren't, I'd have already heard about it. The ones I'm worried about are your mutt and that ugly little cat. I still don't know why they wouldn't let us bring them in the ambulance." Stella brushed the doctor's hand away, pressed the bandage he was trying to apply to her cheek into place.

"There. Done," she said, jumping up from the table, apparently more than ready to leave. "Let's get out of here, Harper."

"If you'll wait a moment, I'll have the nurse come in with aftercare instructions," the doctor said, not even trying to get her to sit down again.

"Don't bother," Stella said blithely. "I'm a nurse, and I'll take good care of the wound."

"But—" the doctor began.

Stella ignored him, grabbing Harper's hand and dragging her into the hallway.

"I could have stitched myself up a lot faster," she said, as if they hadn't been shot at and nearly killed, as if she hadn't just gotten five stitches in her cheek, as if some guy with a gun hadn't been lying dead a hundred yards from the SUV.

Harper had seen him there, facedown, the gun still clutched in his hand.

It had shaken her, brought back those memories of walking into the morgue, bracing herself to do what Gabe wouldn't.

She gagged, and Stella shot her a hard look.

"Pull it together, Harper. This is no time to have a mental breakdown."

"I don't plan on it."

"Good, because you need to call your brother-in-law and get him to drive over here. Since Logan and Malone are occupied with the police, we're in need of a ride, and I can't think of anyone else who can come get us on such short notice."

"Except maybe me?" a man asked, the voice so surprising even Stella jumped.

Harper glanced over her shoulder and saw a tall, stern-looking guy who could have been thirty or forty or somewhere in between. Handsome in a polished way, his dark hair cropped short, his eyes the color of the summer sky.

He smiled as he met Harper's eyes.

"You must be Harper," he said, and she nodded.

"That's right."

"Chance Miller. One of the owners of HEART." He stepped into place beside her, his gaze sliding from her to Stella.

Stella seemed determined to ignore the look. Her gaze was focused on the wide double doors a few feet ahead. From the tension radiating from her, Harper would say she was probably planning a way she could run through them and disappear.

"Nice to meet you, Chance," Harper said. The tension between Chance and Stella was so noticeable, she was tempted to leave them to work out their differences. She might have done it if she weren't worried about Logan and about Malone, and if she'd actually wanted to call Gabe for a ride.

She didn't.

She didn't want to go back to his place, didn't want to look at all those old photos again, didn't want to see Gabe and Maggie together, or think about all the things the two seemed to have that Lydia never would.

Forever. She'd seen that in Gabe's and Maggie's eyes when they'd looked at each other— commitment, affection, the kind of love that lasted.

She'd never seen that between Lydia and Gabe. Ever.

It hadn't been between Harper and Daniel, either.

She could admit that now. All these years later, she could acknowledge that they'd never been meant for each other.

"Wish it were under better circumstances, but I'll be honest." Chance smiled. "Most of the people I meet, I meet during times like this."

"Did Logan call you?" she asked, because she really was worried about him. He'd run off after a guy with a gun as if he did it every day, as if there were nothing to be afraid of, nothing to worry about.

Maybe he did. Maybe there wasn't. But she'd

been afraid and worried, and if it hadn't been for Stella bleeding in the front seat of the SUV, she'd have followed him into the darkness and done whatever she could to help.

"He did. Twenty minutes ago. He needed a ride from the accident scene."

"Accident?" Stella snorted. "That's one way to put it."

"Would you rather me say the scene of the shooting?" Chance responded, not even a hint of irritation in his voice.

"I'd rather you…" Stella's voice trailed off. "You can say whatever you want, boss. I'm tired. Since you're here, I'm catching a cab and going home."

"You want off the case?" he asked, and she frowned.

"This was never a case. I was helping a friend. Now I'm done. Tell Logan he can call me if he needs anything else."

She slammed through the double doors and walked into the emergency room waiting area.

Harper would have gone after her, but Chance touched her arm. "Let her be."

"She just got stitches in her cheek. She might—"

"She's the toughest person I know. She'll be fine," he said. "Logan is talking to Detective

Willard. I told him that I'd find you and bring you to him."

"Detective Willard is here?" The news was like a shot of adrenaline, and she headed toward the doors again.

"This way, Harper." He nudged her back the way they'd come. No bossy maneuvering, none of the macho stuff she'd have expected based on the way Stella acted around him.

There was a story there, but she wasn't nearly as interested in that as she was in the story of the girl in the picture.

They wound their way through the emergency room and walked into a quiet hallway lined with doors. Chance knocked on one. It opened, and Detective Thomas Willard was there—tall, gaunt, his black eyes as solemn and serious as she remembered.

"Harper," he said with a half smile. "It's been a while."

"Yes. It has." She stepped into the room and saw Logan sitting at a long table, a cup of coffee in his hands.

He had pine needles in his hair and a smudge of dirt on his cheek, and when she looked at him, she felt as if she was looking at someone she'd known forever, someone she might want to know for the rest of her life.

Surprised, she stepped back and knocked into Chance.

"We've got a lot to talk about," he said, and she found herself moving forward again, settling into a chair beside Logan, looking into his dark eyes.

"Are you okay?" she asked, the words raspy and a little tight.

"I was going to ask you the same," he responded. "You look tired."

"You look as if you've walked through the forest." She reached out, brushed a few needles from his hair. It was silkier than she'd have thought, and she had to pull back, keep herself from lingering where she shouldn't.

"Just a few pine trees."

"Is Malone okay?"

"He's fine. The police cleared him to go. A coworker drove him to the safe house. He's got Picasso and the kitten with him."

"Things could have been a lot worse," she murmured.

"They could have been," Detective Willard agreed as he took a seat beside her. "I'm not liking what's going on, Harper. Someone has it out for you, and I'd like to know who. I'd also like to know if it's connected to what happened to your sister."

"How could it not be?" she asked.

"It's been four years since your sister's murder. Anything could have happened since then. Do you have a boyfriend? An ex?"

"Not a new one. Just Daniel, and we were over long before Lydia died."

"Coworkers?"

"Detective, I'm going to make this really easy for you," she cut in. "I live by myself. Out in the middle of nowhere. Other than church, I don't go anywhere. I don't hang out with anyone. I've had no deep relationships in four years."

That sounded...pitiful.

"How about people you work with?"

"I'm an artist. The art dealers I supply have never met me. I send my stuff in, and they send me the checks. It's all very simple and impersonal. I don't even use my real name. They don't have my address. Everything is shipped to a PO box, and that's not linked to my old life."

"Old life?" Chance asked, pulling out the chair across from her. He sat, his crisp white shirt wrinkle-free, his jacket stylish and good quality. She had a feeling there was more to him than met the eye, though. He didn't just spend his days pushing papers in an office.

"What I mean," she said, trying to clarify without sounding even more pitiful, "is that I don't have any contact with the people I knew when my sister was alive. I moved away, and I cut my ties."

He nodded as if it made sense.

She wasn't sure it did.

She'd run because she'd had no one to stay for, nothing to hold her back, but that wasn't something she was going to admit. It seemed a sad testament to all the hard work she'd done, all the connections she'd made in the business world, the people she'd gone to lunch with, worked out at the gym with, gone to dinner with.

All those relationships? They'd been as much of a lie as her relationship with Daniel. Not a lie, maybe. But those friendships never had the depth she'd longed for.

Sometimes she wondered if she was capable of that, if she had it in her to have more than her mother and sister had. They'd been surface people, content to jump from relationship to relationship, hobby to hobby, moment to moment.

Harper?

She'd always wanted something more.

"Here's the thing," Detective Willard said, his gruff voice pulling her from things she was better off forgetting. "The FBI is processing the package your brother-in-law received. They've found nothing on the newspaper article. Nothing on the scrap of fabric. No DNA. No hair fibers. Gabe says he's sure the fabric is from Amelia's blanket."

"Wishful thinking?" Logan asked, and Harper found herself looking at him again, meeting his eyes. Her heart leaped, but she ignored it. Told herself she was a fool for letting it happen. Logan was bigger than life, and she was content to live quietly—no fuss, no drama.

"Gabe isn't the kind of person who lets his feelings get the best of him," she said. "He's more likely to be cautious than not, and I don't think he'd say that if he weren't completely convinced. Besides, I thought the blanket was the same, too."

"Sure enough to testify in court?" Logan asked, and she shook her head.

"The pieces do look like they came from Amelia's blanket, but it's been years, and I don't remember exactly what the blanket looked like."

"You were convinced enough to call me," Detective Willard said.

It wasn't a question, but she nodded. "Not just because of the blanket. The package left a bad taste in my mouth. I guess I felt as if someone was purposely trying to prod at the scars, you know? Bring everything to the forefront."

"Seems that what someone really wanted to do was get to you," Detective Willard responded. "But why? It's been four years. If someone wanted you dead, he could have easily come after you before now."

Logan must have been thinking that. He touched her hand, his fingers brushing across her knuckles. "Had anyone called you recently? Any unusual cars driving up to your house and leaving?"

"Not until you showed up," she said, clearing her throat, trying to put herself back in the place where she'd lived for years—the place where pain touched her only a little, where the wounds were scarred over and didn't hurt nearly as much.

"I'm not going to overlook the fact that Gabe was responsible for that," Detective Willard responded as his cell phone buzzed. He took it from his pocket, glanced at the number. "I need to take this. Give me a minute."

He walked out into the hall, leaving Harper with Logan and Chance and the hard knot in her stomach that wouldn't go away.

"We'll head to the safe house when we're done here," Chance said quietly. "Things will be clearer in the morning."

"What things?" Harper asked, standing and pacing across the room. There was a window, the shades closed. She didn't open them. She didn't want to look out at the world—the people moving through the parking lot, the Christmas lights shining from buildings and houses. She didn't want to be reminded that life was going on without Lydia.

"All the things that are worrying you," he said simply. "I don't know about you, but I could use something to eat. I'll go to the cafeteria and pick something up. You vegetarian?"

"No."

"Any allergies?"

"No."

"You're getting her a snack, Chance," Logan said. "I don't think it's a life-and-death situation."

"It could be," Chance replied as he stepped out into the hall.

He closed the door, and she could hear his footsteps retreating. She wanted to follow. Mostly because standing there wasn't accomplishing anything, and she felt the desperate need for action.

"How's Stella?" Logan asked. "Still getting those stitches?"

"She's done, and she wasn't going to hang around waiting for aftercare instructions."

"You mean she wasn't going to stay around Chance?"

"I guess that's true, too."

"They dated for about three minutes. It didn't work out." He moved toward her, tugged her around so they were face-to-face. "That little tidbit of information was supposed to distract you from your troubles. I see it didn't work."

"Did you really think it would?" she asked.

"I knew it wouldn't, but I thought I'd try." He smiled, and she found herself smiling in return.

"I guess I'll appreciate the effort, then. Even if it doesn't change anything."

"What would you like to change?"

"My decision to leave DC? My decision to believe the police when they said Amelia was probably dead? Everything I've done since the moment my sister called me and asked if she could spend the night at my place?"

"Was it the first time she'd asked?"

"No. She and Gabe would have a fight, she'd call me and tell me she was leaving him and needed a place to stay. She'd always leave for a night, and then return. He knew that's what she'd do, and he'd just let her go."

"And you'd never said no to her?"

"Of course not."

"Then, why would that night have been any different?"

"It wouldn't have, but hindsight is twenty-twenty, and I'm always wishing that I'd said no, or that I'd caught her leaving the house with Amelia."

"She didn't tell you they were going?"

"No. She tucked Amelia into bed at eight. Just like she always did. We talked until ten, and then I went to bed. I had a meeting the next morning. An important one." Not that she could remember what had been important about it. "When I got up in the morning, they were both gone."

"You couldn't have changed anything. You know that, right?"

"I don't know anything anymore, Logan. I thought I had it all figured out. I was wrong."

"None of us will ever have life figured out. The best we can do is honor God, honor the people around us and enjoy the time we have," he said gently, his knuckles brushing her cheek, there and gone so quickly, she wasn't sure they'd been there at all.

He was right. She knew that. She would have said it if the door hadn't opened and Detective Willard hadn't walked back in.

The look on his face made the breath catch in Harper's throat, and she found herself reaching for something, anything to hold herself steady. She found Logan's hand, realized what she had and tried to pull away.

He didn't release his hold, just moved up beside her, his shoulder and arm warm against hers. "What's going on?" he asked, and Detective Willard dropped into a chair, his face ashen.

"That was Agent Lawrence with the FBI. A couple of news stations ran late-night previews of the story about Amelia."

"And?" Harper's grip on Logan's hand tightened, everything in the world coming down to that moment and the answer to that one question.

"They got a call from a man in York, Pennsylvania. He said the girl is his daughter."

"So she's not Amelia?" Harper asked, relieved, disappointed, frustrated.

"I didn't say that," Detective Willard replied, the words like lead weights, each one heavier than the next.

"Then, how about you tell me what you did say," Harper suggested. "Because what I thought I heard was that the girl's father called."

"Her father did call. He's a pastor and was at the hospital with a parishioner who had a heart attack last night and needed open-heart surgery."

Get to the point, Harper wanted to shout, but Logan squeezed her hand gently, offering her the support she desperately needed. She kept her mouth shut and waited the detective out.

"He was in the waiting room with the family, and the television was on. They all saw the news story, and they all knew it was his daughter."

"Is that why he called?" Logan asked.

"He called because he's a man of God, and he believes in doing the right thing. His daughter is nine. She's in fourth grade, and she's very bright. Her name is Autumn, but—" he squeezed the bridge of his nose and closed his eyes for a second "—she's always insisted they call her Amelia."

The room shook with that last word, with that name. Or maybe Harper was shaking. Logan nudged her to a chair, and she sat. "I don't understand," she murmured.

"He and his wife adopted her when she was five," Detective Willard explained. "She and her birth mom showed up at church one Sunday. The woman was really thin and sickly looking, so the pastor's wife took her under her wing. Turns out the birth mom had cancer, and she was scared to death that Autumn would be left alone in the world. After a few months, she asked if the pastor and his wife would be willing to adopt her daughter."

"And then she passed away?"

"No. She left. She said she didn't want Autumn to remember her sick and dying. She wanted all her memories to be good ones. They finalized the adoption, and she left town. They never heard from her again. It never occurred to them that the woman might have been lying. She had a birth certificate for Autumn, baby pictures. A death certificate for the man listed as the father. It was all legal as could be."

"Except that it wasn't," Logan said quietly, his hands on Harper's shoulders.

"The father is devastated. His wife is going to be devastated." Detective Willard shook his head. He looked as if he'd aged a dozen years in the past few minutes. "We shouldn't have assumed that Amelia died. We should have kept searching."

"You couldn't have known." Harper offered the platitude by rote. All her thoughts were on the blonde girl with her sister's face.

Amelia.

Lost and found again?

"Amelia would be only eight." She spoke into the silence, that one tiny fact niggling at the back of her mind. "Maybe everything the woman said was the truth. Maybe Autumn was her daughter. Maybe she really was sick."

"Maybe a little girl named Autumn wanted to be called Amelia?" Logan said softly, his hands smoothing along her shoulders, then drifting away. She felt cold in their absence and very, very alone. "It's not a common name, Harper, and I don't believe in coincidence."

"I need to meet the family," she said, pushing away from the table, running to the door. She yanked it open and nearly barreled into Chance.

He stood clutching a white paper bag and a cup holder filled with coffee cups.

She didn't have time to explain.

She needed the truth, and if that meant going to York to get it, that was what she was going to do.

ELEVEN

She needed space. Logan understood that. He also understood that Harper was in danger. The space she craved could very well get her killed.

He followed her through the hospital hallway, keeping some distance between them as she ran into the lobby. People were noticing her. Why wouldn't they? She was beautiful, her hair spilling around her head in thick, wild curls, her eyes wide and haunted. She had a delicate look that belied her tough nature, but even the toughest people could break if they were pushed hard enough.

He thought maybe she had, so he didn't call out to her, didn't tell her to stop. He hoped the need for self-preservation would kick in before she walked outside, but it didn't seem as if that was going to happen.

She reached the door, and he stopped her, snagging the back of her coat and pulling her up short.

"That wouldn't be safe," he said, and she rounded on him, all the fury and frustration she was feeling reflected in the depths of her eyes.

"I really don't care," she countered, yanking her coat from his grasp and turning to the door again.

"Will you care if you die before you reconnect with your niece?"

She was halfway out the door when he said it, and she hesitated there, the cold November air wafting in, carrying a hint of moisture with it.

"She's someone else's daughter, too, Logan. Not just my niece and Lydia and Gabe's daughter. If what that man said is true—"

"We don't know if it is or isn't, and we won't know until the FBI verifies the story. For right now, let's just take things a step at a time."

"What steps?" she asked, finally stepping back inside and letting the door close. "What steps can ever lead us to a good reconciliation with this? Everyone is going to lose. You know that, right? If the couple truly believed they were adopting Amelia from her dying mother, if they've raised her for four years, loved her for four years—"

"You're borrowing trouble," he said, cutting her off before she could go any further.

"I know. I do. But… I just never expected this. Even when I got that package, when I saw the blanket, even then I didn't think anything like this could be true. I just thought someone was taunting me, trying to hurt me for some reason."

"The reality is worse, Harper. Someone knew what happened to Amelia and used that knowledge to bring you out of hiding."

"I wasn't hiding. Not really." She brushed a few strands of hair from her cheek, her hand shaking.

"No?" He touched her lower back, moving her the way they'd come, through the lobby and into the emergency room waiting area. It seemed safer there, but he knew it wasn't. The deeper he got into this case, the more he thought everything that was happening was about revenge or anger or hatred. It was all too personal to be anything else. All too plotted out and connected. The package sent to Gabe, the one sent to Harper, the little hints at what could be. Whoever was responsible had a message to deliver, and Logan didn't think it had anything to do with Amelia.

"If I'd wanted to hide," Harper said as they moved through the emergency department, "I'd have moved a lot farther away. I'd have closed out that PO box, and I'd have changed my name. All I really wanted to do was…" She didn't continue, just rubbed the back of her neck and sighed.

"What did you want to do?" he prodded, because he wanted to know.

"The truth?" She stopped short, looked straight into his eyes. "I wanted to find out what life was really about, because it sure wasn't about the job I'd worked so hard for or the people I saw for a couple of minutes every day. It wasn't about money or stability or having a lot of nice things. It wasn't about any of the stuff I'd thought it was about when I was a kid. Seeing my sister's body lying in a morgue? It made me realize I'd spent a lot of years chasing after the wrong things. I left because I wanted to figure out what I should be chasing after."

"Did you?"

She smiled at the question, her eyes tinged with sadness. "I guess I did. I realized that life wasn't about chasing anything. It was about living. I wish I could have told my sister that." She started walking again, her legs long and lean, her shoulders narrow. She looked more like an athlete than an artist, but he'd seen her work. He knew how much vision she had for it, the swirled paint and simple designs that seemed to reflect every color nature had to offer.

"If you had, would she have listened?" They'd reached the room where Chance and Detective

Willard waited, but he didn't open the door, and she didn't, either.

"I don't think so," she said. "Lydia was a little larger than life. She wanted the best and the brightest and the most beautiful things. Usually she got them."

"And you?"

"Me, what?"

"What did you want?"

"Just what most people want—happiness, contentment, maybe a little peace."

"You didn't have those things?"

"Not when I was a kid. When I was an adult… I guess I didn't appreciate them. Let's go make our plan, because if we don't do it soon, I really am going to take off on my own, go to York, track down the pastor and his wife and Amelia and figure all this out myself." She opened the door and walked into the room. He followed, her words ringing in his ears.

Happiness.

Contentment.

Peace.

He knew what it was like to want those things. He'd longed for them during the years he'd been raising his brothers.

Finishing their raising.

That was how they always put it.

Logan felt different. Or he had at the time.

He'd felt as if he was sacrificing a lot to give his brothers what his parents would have wanted them to have.

It had all turned out fine in the end, but there'd been times when he'd wanted to throw in the towel and call it quits. Even more times when he'd longed for the things Harper had mentioned.

Simple things, but important ones.

Maybe she could pursue them once she found her niece, or maybe she'd figure out that she'd had them all along.

It seemed to him that someone living the way she had must know a thing or two about a simple existence, about appreciation for what she had, about contentment and peace.

He stepped into the room behind her and was surprised to see Malone standing near the window.

"I thought you were at the safe house," he said, and Malone scowled.

"Was. Then Stella showed up and told me she'd take animal-sitting duties."

"Stella doesn't call the shots," Chance said, a slight edge to his voice. "I do."

"You want me to leave, tell me to. Otherwise, how about we just focus on what needs doing?"

"Meaning a trip to Pennsylvania?" Detective

Willard broke in. "Because if that's what you're planning, it's out of the question."

"Since when is traveling across state lines out of the question?" Chance asked conversationally. Which meant he was royally irritated by the detective's pronouncement.

"This isn't about a simple trip, Mr. Miller. This is about interfering with an ongoing investigation."

"It's about finding my niece, and I'm not willing to sit around and wait for other people to do that," Harper spoke up, her tone firm.

"I'm afraid you're going to have to."

"I'm afraid you're going to have to lock me in jail if that's what you want me to do, because there's no way it's going to happen otherwise," Harper retorted, and Logan knew she meant every word.

She was going to find the pastor and his wife.

One way or another.

"I'm not trying to keep you from your niece," Detective Willard shot back. "I'm trying to keep you alive. I couldn't do that for your sister, but I can do it for you. So you're staying put until the pastor's story is verified. Once it is, I'll make arrangements for you to be escorted to York."

"That could take weeks," she protested, and the detective shrugged.

"I'll let you know as soon as I've got everything cleared." He stood and walked to the door, pausing there to shoot Chance a hard look. "I suggest your organization stay out of this one, Mr. Miller. I know you mean well, but we've got protocol to follow, and getting in the way of that could cause problems."

"Understood," Chance responded, his voice tight, his expression tighter. He didn't like being told what to do, but he wouldn't buck the system. He and his brother Jackson had spent too much time building HEART. The team had put too much energy into preserving its reputation. That was what got them into places others couldn't go. It was what allowed them to move across borders. Without that, they were nothing.

With it, they were trapped, forced to work closely with local police, follow their orders and respect their boundaries.

Right at that moment, Logan wasn't too happy about that.

"Good," Detective Willard said, seeming satisfied. No one else in the room was. Logan watched as the detective assured Harper that he'd keep her updated, said his goodbyes and left.

"Well," Malone drawled, snagging the white bag that had been abandoned on the table. "That went well."

"It went just fine, and the food is for Harper." Chance grabbed the bag and handed it to Harper.

"Fine?" She opened the bag, then closed it again. "If *fine* means that we're all going to sit around twiddling our thumbs, then fine isn't acceptable to me."

"I don't believe in twiddling my thumbs." Chance pulled out his cell phone and texted someone.

"Then, what do you believe in?" she asked.

"God. Family. Friends." He paused, glanced at his phone and grinned. "And finding my way around protocol. Let's head over to the safe house. We'll come up with a plan there."

Harper had no desire to go to the safe house, and she didn't care squat about working around protocol. She had absolutely nothing to lose, and she was more than ready to head to York *now*, not an hour or two or ten from now.

Somehow she ended up in Chance's car anyway. Found herself squeezed between Logan and Malone. Again.

No Picasso this time. No kitten. No Stella.

Just three men, discussing ETAs and worst-case scenarios and a bunch of other things that she only barely paid attention to. She was more interested in the texts Gabe was sending her. One after another after another. Telling her that he'd been contacted by the FBI. Asking if she'd heard the news. Asking if she thought it could be true. Asking where she was and when she planned to return to his place.

Never.

She almost sent that, but she thought better of it.

She typed *I don't know* instead, pressed Send and waited for the next text to come through.

Seconds later, it did:

Where are you heading?

To—

Logan snatched the phone from her hands. Surprising, because she'd had no idea he was paying any attention to what she was doing.

"Not a good idea to answer that, Harper," he said.

"You could have just said so instead of taking my phone." She held out her hand, but he didn't give it back.

"Usually, people at our safe houses aren't allowed to keep their phones. They can be tracked pretty easily that way."

"Going to the safe house wasn't my idea. I don't think I need to follow the rules for it."

"Actually," Chance cut in, "you do. We use

this place a few times a year, and I'd hate for it to be compromised."

"I won't tell Gabe where I'm going."

"You don't have to say a word. The phone will say everything for you." Logan switched it off and held it out to her. "Keep it off until we're on the road again."

"I don't like being ordered around, Logan."

"I don't like being shot at, but it happens all the time."

That made her laugh, the sound bubbling up and spilling out before she knew it was happening.

"There," he said, smiling through the darkness. "That's better."

"What?"

"You were wound up so tight, I thought you'd bust. Now you're looking more relaxed."

"Maybe so, but I still don't like being ordered around." She shoved the cell phone into her pocket and eyed the dark road that stretched out in front of them. "And I'm not really happy about going to the safe house."

"I know."

"So how about we turn around and go back to the city? I can rent a car, head out on my own. That'll keep all of you from getting into trouble and keep me from going insane."

"This won't take long, and it'll be worth it," Logan assured her.

"How is waiting going to be worth it?"

"I have a friend who works for the FBI. He's clearing things for us," Chance responded. "Give him a little more time, and you'll have a private invitation to cross the Penn state border and head to the pastor's house."

"You know where that is?" she asked, her heart jumping, her pulse racing.

"Not yet, but I will, and once I do, we'll be clear to go." He pulled off the main road, heading down a narrow dirt path that led through thick trees. Branches scraped the top of the car and scratched at the windows, but Chance didn't seem bothered by it.

They bounced up a hill, down it, the woods opening into a wide clearing, an old farmhouse sitting smack-dab in the middle of it. A lone light shone from one window. Other than that, the place looked empty and not all that inviting.

"Finally," Malone muttered as they pulled up in front. "I'm taking a nap. You hash everything out. Wake me up when we're ready to actually do something."

He was out of the car and in the house before Harper could unhook her seat belt.

"Sleeping is probably a good idea. You look exhausted," Logan said as he opened his door.

"That's like the pot calling the kettle black."

He chuckled, getting out of the car and offering her a hand. She took it, the warmth of his palm sending a shiver of longing through her—longing for all those things she'd wanted an eon ago, all the things she'd been so certain she'd have with Daniel.

She moved away, wiping her palm against her jeans as if somehow that could wipe away the warmth lingering where his hand had been.

He noticed, his dark gaze dropping to her thigh, a half smile curving his lips. "You can ignore it for a while longer," he whispered in her ear as they made their way up rickety porch stairs. "But then you're going to have to face it."

"I don't know what you're talking about."

"Sure you do," he said, urging her into the house.

The place was nicer on the inside than it was on the outside, the walls painted a subtle buttery yellow, the wainscoting bright white. There were no pictures on the walls, no rugs on the floors. Just an old-world charm that made her think of simpler times.

"It's nice," she said to no one in particular.

"Nice enough for a few hours of rest and regrouping, that's for sure." Chance closed the door, locked and bolted it. There were security cameras hanging from the corners of the ceiling, and Harper imagined there were more outside.

She ignored them the same way she was avoiding Logan.

"My friend probably won't hear from his supervisor until the office opens. How about you get some rest while we're waiting?" Chance suggested. "There's a bedroom upstairs. Several of them, actually, but the one right at the top of the stairs is decked out for a guest—clothes in the drawers, and some should fit you. Soap and shampoo in the bathroom. You need anything else, let me know and I'll make sure you get it."

She would have refused, but she could feel the weight of Logan's stare, could still hear his words echoing through her head.

He'd been right, of course. She'd known exactly what he was talking about, and she'd known he was right. At some point, she was going to have to acknowledge what she felt every time she was near him. At some point, she was going to think about what that meant, what it could mean, if both of them wanted it to.

At some point, she'd have to do that, but right now she was going to use Chance's offer as the perfect excuse to do what she wanted—run.

"Thanks," she mumbled, not daring to look at Logan. "I think I'll do that."

Then she took off up the stairs, ran into the first room she saw, closed the door and locked it.

TWELVE

Four hours, five minutes and fifteen seconds.

Sixteen.

Seventeen.

Harper watched the hands of an old clock on the wall and counted the amount of time that she'd been lying on a bed, waiting for…something.

She wasn't even sure what she was waiting for.

Not for someone to knock on the door and ask if she was okay.

That had happened about five minutes after she'd locked herself in. It had been Logan, of course. He'd knocked twice after that. Both times she'd told him she was fine. Both times he'd walked away. Left her to deal with things the way she wanted.

Which was good. Great, even.

She hadn't wanted to talk to Logan or Chance or Malone. She hadn't wanted to listen to Stella imply that hiding in her room was the easy thing to do.

She already knew that, and she was still doing it, because she did not want to face Logan or her fears or the knowledge that her niece was out in the world, and she was sitting around waiting for permission to go visit her.

Too much. All of it.

And so she'd run into the room and locked the door and willed herself to sleep, but sleep hadn't come. She'd just lain there staring at the clock, wondering how long it would take for a dozen things she wanted to happen actually to happen. Picasso had nosed at the door, whining softly. She would have let him in, but some-one called him, the gruff voice either Logan's or Malone's.

The house had grown silent.

The sun had risen.

No voices. No people moving up and down stairs or through the hallway outside the door. Just her and every thought she didn't want to think about her niece, her sister.

And Logan.

She eyed the clock. Four hours. Six minutes. Nine seconds.

If she lay there one more minute, she'd go nuts.

She jumped up and opened one of the dresser

drawers. There were clothes there. Lots of them—brand-new jeans, brand-new T-shirts, sweatshirts and sweaters with the tags still on. She grabbed something that looked as if it would fit, walked into the attached bathroom and took a quick shower.

It did nothing to cheer her mood.

If someone had told her a week ago that her niece was alive, she wouldn't have believed it. Now she couldn't stop thinking about Amelia and the possibility that she was alive, living with a couple in York, Pennsylvania.

Possibility?

It seemed like a certainty.

I don't believe in coincidence.

That was what Logan had said, and she agreed. It was too much of a stretch to think that a nine-year-old girl—eight?—would arbitrarily decide she wanted her name to be Amelia.

Autumn/Amelia had told the pastor and his wife her name. Had she told them about her old life? The one she'd lived in the fancy house in DC, with the blonde mother who was larger than life?

Had she told them about the murder?

About being taken from everything she'd loved?

Had they brushed off her concerns, chalked the stories up to an overactive imagination?

Or had they somehow been involved in her kidnapping?

Harper walked to one of the windows, pulled back the curtains and opened the blinds. The day had dawned, thick layers of clouds covering the sun and pressing close over trees and distant houses.

If she'd been home, she'd have gone outside with Picasso and her bucket, gathered clay in preparation for the winter. That chore, the one she'd been working on so diligently as late summer and fall arrived, seemed part of another life, and she wondered how she'd go back to it. The routine of finding the perfect clay, preparing it, throwing it onto a wheel? It didn't seem nearly as consuming as it had the previous day.

A selfish life.

The thought flashed through her mind, and she tried to push it away. There was nothing selfish about what she'd been doing. There'd been no one who needed her, nothing that she'd left behind unfinished or neglected.

Maybe, though, there'd been a lot she could have done with the past four years. Not that she wasn't proud of the art she'd created and the name she'd made for herself. She'd redefined herself after she'd lost her job, and that was something she stood behind, but what else had she done?

Hidden? From life? From the complications it brought?

The thought didn't fill her with good cheer and happiness. There were so many things that she could have done. Even at the small church she attended, there were people in need—elderly people who had no one, young mothers who would have loved a few hours a week to themselves. Harper didn't have family, but she could have made some friends if she'd wanted to.

She'd been too hurt, too sad and too certain that it would all turn out the way it had before—dust in the wind, scattering here and there and impossible to gather up. Just memories of a few fun times and some sad ones.

She was a coward.

Even now, she had looked into Logan's eyes and seen exactly what she'd been feeling—interest and attraction and a little bit of hope—but she'd been too scared to do anything with that, too worried about what she might lose to reach out and try to take anything. As if, somehow, she knew better than God what her life would be. As if, somehow, she understood the path she was on better than He understood it.

She moved away from the window, shoved her feet into her shoes and unlocked the door, disgusted with herself. She'd been hiding for a lot of years, but she wasn't going to hide anymore. Her niece was alive, and she deserved to be found, to be comforted and to be offered as much information as she could handle.

Eight was young to have her life turned upside down again, but maybe Amelia had always known it would happen. Maybe the memories were still alive and well, and maybe she'd be happy to have her father and aunt in her life again.

Maybe.

One way or another, the truth was going to come out, secrets were going to be revealed and someone wasn't going to be happy about it.

Who?

That was the question Harper couldn't answer.

She'd have thought Gabe. He was the easiest one to point the finger at. Maybe he'd secreted his daughter away, hidden her until he could bring her home and make it seem as if they were both victims of a crime.

But that didn't sit right with Harper. Gabe had never been much of an actor. His feelings were always there for the world to see. He didn't hide them and he didn't apologize for them—anger, frustration, irritation, impatience. She'd seen them all flash across his face on more than one occasion. And she'd seen his grief at the funeral. She'd seen the tears.

Was it possible he'd faked them?

She doubted it. She really did.

And yet, someone had arranged all of this—Lydia's death, Amelia's kidnapping. It hadn't been random. It must have been carefully planned out and executed. Four years had passed, and not one person had suspected Amelia was alive. Someone had wanted it that way. And then someone hadn't.

Why?

She stepped into the hall and walked down old wooden steps, the soft creaks and groans reminding her of the old apartment buildings she'd lived in when she was a kid. Ten or fifteen different places, one after another, because they'd been evicted over and over again. Her mother hadn't been able to keep money in her pocket. If she had it, she gave it to whatever guy she was with at the time, or she spent it on makeup and creams and hair products to attract the next guy.

Not a good memory, but she had loved her daughters.

There'd been no doubt about that.

It hadn't been a stable love or a productive one, but she'd given what she could. Lydia had done the same with Amelia, offering her even more than she'd had. If there was any success in their family, it was that.

Harper jogged down the last few steps and turned down a hallway that stretched the width of the house. The hallway opened into a large kitchen—stainless-steel appliances, granite counters, beautiful wood flooring. All of it updated and spotless. A coffeemaker sat on the counter. She checked the filter and plugged it in, her heart thudding hollowly in her chest. Going through the motions of a morning routine didn't change anything. Her entire life had been turned upside down. So had Gabe's. So had Amelia's. So had the couple's who'd adopted her.

Harper opened the fridge. Someone had stocked it, but she wasn't hungry. She grabbed creamer and was setting it on the counter when Picasso bounded into the room. He went straight to a giant bowl that someone had set near the back door, nosed the emptiness and gave her the eye.

"What?" she asked, scratching him behind the ears. "I don't have any food for you."

"Under the sink," Logan said, his voice so surprising she jumped.

She whirled to face him, her heart jumping as she looked into his dark eyes. "I…didn't hear you."

"The sound of your giant puppy masked my

approach," he responded. He looked as if he'd just woken up, his hair mussed, his clothes a little wrinkled, his eyes bleary.

"I guess I wasn't as quiet as I thought. Sorry for waking you."

"I had to be up anyway." He took two mugs from a cupboard, set sugar beside them. "Everything has been arranged. We're meeting Chance's friend in an hour. He's going to escort us to the church where Amelia's adoptive family is waiting."

"Is she there?" she asked, her hand shaking as she poured steaming coffee into both mugs.

"No. Everyone thought it was best if she go to school and continue about her day without knowing anything about this."

"Her face was all over the news. She's going to hear from someone."

"The FBI had the story pulled once her…once the pastor called them. I doubt any of the kids at her school saw it. If they did, the pastor and his wife will deal with it."

"If they aren't in jail," she murmured, spooning sugar into her coffee, pouring creamer.

"They won't be going to jail." He took his coffee black, sipping it as steam drifted from the mug. "Everything the pastor said checked out. Dozens of people from his congregation were interviewed. They all confirmed the story."

"That makes things even harder, I think," she said, setting her mug on the counter. Her stomach was in knots, and she didn't think she could drink the coffee.

"It complicates them, that's for sure."

"I wonder how Gabe is handling it," she said as she poured dog kibble into Picasso's bowl and put kitten food in another smaller bowl that was sitting nearby.

"You're going to find out. He's coming to Pennsylvania with us."

"Wow," she said, because it was all she could think. Three days ago, she'd been collecting clay, not thinking about anything but the next art show, the next project. Gabe had been planning a wedding...

"Does it seem strange to you," she asked, "that all of this is happening right before Gabe's wedding?"

"Strange?" He pulled out a chair and urged her into it, his arm skimming her shoulder as he leaned to set the mug on the table. "Convenient, maybe."

"How so?"

He settled into the chair beside her, took another sip of coffee. His eyes were brighter now, but his hair still looked mussed from sleep. She wanted to run her hand over it, smooth strands the way she had when he'd had pine needles stuck there.

She grabbed the coffee instead, chugged down the sugary brew.

"Gabe's daughter was dead. Now he's getting married and she's alive again. He can bring her home and settle her back into the house with his new wife. A woman who will probably be a great mother."

That hurt. Thinking about Lydia being replaced by Maggie, thinking about Maggie moving into the house Lydia had taken so much pride in—it was like a blow to the heart.

"I'm sorry." Logan took her hand and gave it a gentle squeeze. "I shouldn't have said all that."

"It's okay. It's the truth." She could have pulled her hand away, but she didn't. It felt too nice to sit there with Logan, their coffee mugs abandoned on the table, Picasso lying at their feet. It felt too much like all the things she'd wanted when she'd been young and naive enough to think she could have them.

"A truth that didn't need to be spoken this early in the morning. Did you sleep at all?" he asked, changing the subject.

It was for the best.

There was nothing more that could be added. Until they met with the FBI, Gabe and the couple who'd adopted Amelia, they wouldn't have a clear picture of what had happened.

"No, but I thought a lot."

"About?"

"The way I hid for four years. I could have done a lot for many people during that time. Instead, I just kept to myself."

"You needed time to heal," he said, smoothing his hair the way she'd wanted to.

There was something about him—something gruff and rough and compelling that made her want to stare into his eyes, hear what he had to say, listen the way she'd always wanted to be listened to—as if every word were important, every thought mattered.

"I wish that had been my motivation," she said. "It wasn't, and I'd be lying if I said otherwise. The truth is, too many people wanted too much from me—stories about Lydia, interviews about my involvement in her disappearance. Tears over the loss of my niece and sister. I didn't want to give them anything. I figured they already had enough, were already making a mockery of her life and her death. Their lives and deaths. Only Amelia..."

"Wasn't dead," he finished, and she lifted her mug, took a long swallow. Too sweet, but she wasn't going to add more coffee to it. She didn't think her shaking hands could manage it.

Picasso bounded up from his place on the floor, ran to the doorway that led into the hall and stood there, tail wagging.

Someone else must be awake.

It was for the best.

There were a million words Harper could say, and she had a feeling Logan would listen to all of them, but there was more that needed to be done than talking. Questions that needed to be answered, secrets that needed to be revealed.

Whose secrets?

Not Amelia's adoptive parents'.

Gabe's?

She didn't think so.

Maggie's?

She'd been in the picture four years ago.

"We'll figure it out," Logan said as if he'd read her mind.

"Figure what out?" Malone stepped into the room, the kitten in his arms. He set it on the floor and walked straight to the coffeepot. "What we're eating for breakfast?"

"Grab something quickly." Chance moved into the room behind him. "It's a thirty-minute drive, and if we're late, we'll be left behind."

That was enough to get Harper moving. "I'll take Picasso—"

"Stella is staying here. She'll take care of the dog. All you need to do is be ready to leave."

Chance's tone was smooth, his words even, but there was something hard in his eyes.

She didn't think she'd want to buck his orders, didn't think she'd want to get on his bad side, either.

"I'll grab my phone," she said, sprinting out of the kitchen and up to her room.

A Christmas CD blasted cheerful music into Special Agent Arnold Smith's van, the sound like nails on a chalkboard to Logan. He didn't ask the guy to turn the music off or down. Agent Smith was doing all of them a favor driving them to York to meet Amelia's parents, and Logan didn't want to get on his bad side.

Besides, he loved Christmas. He just wasn't too keen on overly cheerful Christmas music. Especially when he didn't feel cheerful.

Which…he didn't.

He felt anxious, worried. Neither was productive and neither would help him keep Harper safe.

Something that everyone seemed to have lost sight of.

In their hurry to find out what had happened to Amelia, how she'd wound up with a woman who'd claimed to be her mother, the police and FBI seemed to have forgotten that someone wanted Harper dead.

Logan hadn't.

He glanced in the backseat and saw that she'd leaned her head against the window, had her eyes closed.

She wasn't sleeping. Her body was too tense for that. Maybe she was avoiding looking at her brother-in-law and Maggie, holding hands beside her.

Their relationship bothered her. No matter what she'd said.

She must have sensed his gaze. She opened her eyes and offered a sad smile.

"Cheerful music," she commented.

"Matches the cookies Sandra sent for Amelia," Maggie commented, lifting the plastic container she'd been clutching the entire trip. Dozens of colorfully frosted sugar cookies were inside. Apparently, they'd once been Amelia's favorite Christmas cookies, and Sandra had wanted to make certain she had some. That was what Maggie had said. Gabe hadn't said anything. He'd climbed into the backseat and sat silently for the entire trip.

"They are...cheerful and sweet. I'm sure Amelia will love them."

"If her parents allow her to have sugar," Maggie responded, and Gabe stiffened.

"*I'm* her parent. *We'll* be her parents once we're married."

"I know. It's just, they have feelings, too. They love her, too."

"You're making assumptions," he said wearily, and Maggie sighed.

"I'd rather assume the best than the worst, but I guess we'll figure it out when we get there."

"I hope so," Gabe responded, and Maggie touched his cheek, whispered something in his ear.

Harper met Logan's eyes, her skin pale. Maggie had foisted one of the cookies on her a half hour ago, but other than that, he didn't think she'd eaten since sometime the previous day.

"Maybe you should have another one of those cookies," he suggested, and she frowned.

"I didn't even want the first one. I only ate it because everyone was commenting on how pale I looked and telling me I needed energy for the trip."

"Everyone was correct," he said, and she shrugged.

"What I need are answers. And," she added, "maybe a little less Christmas music."

"My kid's CD," Agent Smith said. He'd picked them up at a rest stop a half hour from the safe house with Gabe and Maggie already in the backseat. He'd followed protocol, checked everything out with his supervisor. The police and FBI in Pennsylvania were expecting them. So were Amelia's adoptive parents.

"I don't suppose you have any other options for music?" Logan asked, and Agent Smith sighed.

"If only. My wife shoved it in the player, and we haven't been able to get it out. Planned to bring it in to have it looked at, but this came up."

"I appreciate you helping us out," Chance said from his place in the far back of the vehicle.

"I owe you. More than one. Besides, I have a nine-year-old. If she were missing, I'd do everything in my power to find her. Here's our exit. We'll be there in five. If you look to the left, you'll see the steeple of the church. The white one?"

Logan could see it, white against gray sky and faded fall colors. The town was small, the roads narrow, but Agent Smith seemed to have the route memorized. He turned onto a side road, then another, and followed a winding road uphill.

The church was there, the parking lot dotted with cars—two Pennsylvania State patrol cars. Three unmarked sedans. A tired-looking station wagon with wood-panel sides.

The pastor's car?

The building itself wasn't much to look at— old clapboard siding painted bright white. Simple but well kept. No fancy stained glass. No tall doors or shiny finishes. It reminded Logan of his home church. Not the one he attended in DC, but the one he'd grown up in. The one where everyone knew everyone. Where meals were prepared for families every time a baby was born, a person got sick, a loved one was lost.

"So this is it," Harper murmured, her voice faint.

"This is it," Gabe said, opening the door and stepping out. He helped Maggie from the middle seat and didn't bother waiting for anyone else.

Logan couldn't say he blamed the guy.

This was about his daughter, a child he'd thought he'd lost.

Harper scrambled out after him, ignoring Logan's command for her to wait.

He wasn't surprised by that, either.

He jumped out of the vehicle, winter air slapping his cheeks. Someone had hung a wreath from the church door, and it swayed listlessly as Gabe yanked the door open and went inside.

Maggie grabbed the door before it could close and held it open as Harper walked through. She smiled, but Logan didn't think Harper noticed. Her attention was focused straight ahead. The sleeves of her too-big sweater fell over her hands, but he was pretty sure she'd fisted them and that her short nails were digging crescents into her skin. She stumbled, and he cupped her elbow, worried about her pallor.

"I'm okay," she mumbled, but the words were thick and a little slurred. He wanted to stop, take a closer look at her face, into her eyes. She seemed...off. Not quite steady on her feet. She'd barely slept the night before. He knew that. He'd heard her pacing in her room long after he'd bedded down for the night. Still, this was the kind of situation that would send adrenaline zipping through the most exhausted person. She seemed to have none, her feet dragging as they walked through a wide vestibule and into a quiet sanctuary.

Like the exterior of the church, the interior was simple. Scuffed wood floors that had probably been put down a century ago, dark wood pews padded with faux red velvet cushions. The pulpit stood on a stage that had probably been added long after the building was erected, the simple wood podium and a small altar table the only adornments.

A small group of people stood just in front of the stage. Three men in dark suits. A woman in the same. Three uniformed police officers were there, too, all of them a little stiff, a little tense.

And then there was the man and woman dressed in casual clothes, their faces ashen. The woman leaned heavily on the man, her dark hair swept away from a pretty face. Midthirties, maybe, her long skirt and fitted sweater skimming over a trim athletic figure. The man had a heavier build and the kind of muscle that came from working outdoors. He looked a little older—maybe forty. Or maybe life had just been harder on him.

They both seemed frozen as Gabe walked toward them, the woman visibly shrinking with every step he took.

The pastor and his wife. There was no doubt about that. Nor was there any doubt about the anguish they were experiencing.

The man moved forward, extended his hand. "Pastor Camden Stanley. This is my wife, Hannah."

"Gabe Wilson. Amelia's father," Gabe said, and Maggie grabbed his arm, shot him a warning look.

He didn't seem interested in heeding it. He looked angry, his jaw set. "And I'd like her back. Now. Not a few hours from now."

"Mr. Wilson." One of the FBI agents stepped forward. "We understand your feelings, but this is a delicate situation."

"Delicate how? My daughter was taken from me. These people have no legal right to her."

"Gabe!" Maggie cut in. "We agreed—"

"I agreed that I'd be reasonable. Reasonable

is being reunited with the child who was taken from me."

"The child who has been our daughter for four years," the pastor said, his arm around his wife's waist. She was leaning so hard against him, Logan thought she might fall over.

"The child who was never your daughter," Gabe spat, and tears slipped down Hannah's face, a quiet keening rising up from somewhere so deep inside that it took a minute for Logan to realize the sound was coming from her.

Gabe blinked, all the anger seeping out of his face. "I'm sorry. That was about the worst thing I could say to either of you. I'm upset."

Hannah nodded, but the tears just kept coming.

One of the officers put a hand on her shoulder. "Hannah, how about you sit down and I'll get you some water?"

"I don't need water," she cried. "I just need this nightmare to end."

She allowed herself to be led to a pew, and Maggie crouched next to her, murmuring something as she lifted her wrist and checked her pulse. Chance, Malone and Agent Smith stood a few feet away, watching with a mixture of sympathy and frustration. There was nothing anyone could do. No comfort that could be offered. Even the federal agents, dressed in their suits and polished shoes, looked ill at ease. There was no protocol for this, no script that they could go by. Somehow, Camden and Hannah had ended up with Gabe's daughter. They'd raised her for four years, had obviously loved her and thought of her as their own.

Gabe moved stiffly, crouching next to Maggie and reaching for Hannah's hand.

"We'll work it out," he said. Just those words, and the tension broke. The police started talking, agents started talking, Chance and Malone leaned closer to speak with each another.

And that was when Logan realized something was wrong with Harper. Really wrong. She hadn't moved, didn't speak. Just stood beside him, her skin pale and waxy, her eyes glazed.

"Harper?" he said.

Her gaze shifted, her lips moved, and then she fell, tumbling so quickly, he barely had time to catch her.

He lowered her to the floor, touched her cheek. "Harper?"

She didn't move, didn't respond at all.

He touched the pulse point in her neck, felt her heartbeat. It was thready and light beneath his finger.

"Call an ambulance!" he shouted as Maggie rushed to his side, the cookies she'd been holding dropping to the floor.

Chance knelt beside him.

"We need Stella," he said quietly, and Logan knew it was as bad as he'd thought.

He brushed a strand of hair from Harper's pale cheek, and her eyelids fluttered. He thought she tried to smile, and then she was gone again, and all he could do was pray that help would arrive quickly.

THIRTEEN

Voices. Words. A song that Harper knew but couldn't name.

They drifted into the darkness, nudged her back to consciousness and pain. Head pounding. Stomach aching. Muscles throbbing.

Sick?

She opened her eyes, her stomach twisting in protest as she looked up at a tile ceiling.

"Finally," someone murmured, and memories rushed in, filled the empty places.

Logan.

He sat beside her, his jaw dark with the beginnings of a beard, his eyes deeply shadowed. He looked good—better than anyone had the right to when he was sitting…

Where?

She eyed the small table to his right, the plastic pitcher of water sitting on it, a cup beside it. Behind him, a window looked out onto the cloudy day.

Not the safe house.

They'd left that, but she couldn't seem to catch hold of her thoughts, couldn't quite seem to put memories together.

"What happened?" she tried to ask, but the words stuck in her throat, the aching pain there making her lift her hand, touch her neck.

She had an IV in the back of her hand, tape pressed firmly over the flesh.

A hospital?

Was she sick?

She sure didn't feel well.

"It's okay," Logan said. "You're okay."

"What happened?" This time the words escaped, raspy and rough, but there.

"Poison," he responded, his expression grim, his hand gentle as he brushed strands of hair from her cheek. "The cookie."

She reached for the memory—the trip to DC. Gabe. Maggie. Sandra. The safe house.

Amelia.

And…yes…the cookie. Red frosting on sugary dough because everyone had said she was pale and looked as if she needed to eat. Maggie had said it more loudly than anyone, opening the plastic container and handing Harper the cookie, which had tasted like sugar and sawdust.

Her stomach heaved, and she sat up, her heart pounding frantically in her chest.

"It's okay. Just take a deep breath." Logan touched her nape, his fingers warm, his skin callused, his eyes filled with concern and compassion and a dozen other things she'd never expected to see in a man's gaze.

"Maggie?" she asked.

"She's in custody, insisting she didn't do it, but she had an open bottle of antifreeze in her car. That's what you were poisoned with."

"Cars and antifreeze go together," she said, still fuzzy headed, still not quite sure how she'd ended up where she was.

The cookie.

The church.

The woman's keening sob…

What had her name been?

Hannah?

"Harper? Don't drift away again," Logan said, his words ruffling the hair near her ear, his hand still resting on her neck.

"I'm not," she said. "I'm just trying to figure it out."

"We all are."

"Maggie… She put antifreeze in the cookies?"

"That's what the police are saying," he responded, but there was something in his face, in his eyes, that made her question it.

"What are you saying?"

"*We're* saying that the doctor being thrown in jail is really convenient," someone cut in, the voice sharp and gruff. Malone? She glanced past Logan and saw his coworker sitting in a chair near the door, legs stretched out, ankles crossed, his gun holster strapped across his chest.

"To who?" Harper asked.

"I'm thinking two people—that brother-in-law of yours and his assistant."

"Gabe wouldn't hurt his own daughter," she responded, thinking about those cookies—the bright colors, the sprinkles, all of it so perfectly child friendly.

"Who says he was trying to? You're the only one who ate a cookie. The rest ended up on the floor of the church," Malone said, standing and stretching. "Tell you what. I'm going to grab some coffee. You want anything?"

She wasn't sure if he was talking to her or to Logan, but she shook her head. Her stomach burned and ached. Her head was pounding. The last thing she wanted was food.

The first thing she wanted was the truth.

"Where is Gabe?" she asked as Malone walked out of the room.

"Despite what Malone thinks, he didn't poison anything or anyone. The police questioned him. He submitted to a lie detector test. He passed with flying colors. He's over at the Stanleys'," Logan responded. "With Amelia."

That was it. All she needed to hear. She shoved at the blankets piled on top of her, swung her legs over the side of the bed.

"Whoa! Where do you think you're going?" Logan asked, putting his hand on her shoulder and holding her in place.

If she hadn't felt dizzy and a little too weak, she'd have shoved it away.

"I want to see her."

"You will."

"When?"

"Once the doctor releases you."

"I would like that to be now," she ground out, the quick staccato beat of the words pounding through her already throbbing head.

"There are a lot of things that I'd like, Harper," he responded. "I'm not getting any of them anytime soon, so how about you just relax and accept things the way they are?"

"Because I've never been good at relaxing, and I don't like things this way," she replied, and he chuckled, pressing the call button on the bed railing and settling back into the chair.

"Grumpy when you don't feel good, huh? I'll keep that in mind for the future."

"What future?" she muttered, setting her feet

on cold tile and trying to decide if she had the energy to stand.

She was afraid she didn't, and she was afraid if she went down, Logan would pick her up and set her on the bed, his warm arms and dark, masculine scent wrapping around her for just long enough to give her ideas that she probably shouldn't have—ideas about long walks and longer conversations, about time spent getting to know someone who wanted to get to know her. About all the things she'd thought she'd have with Daniel and had given up on.

"Whatever future we're heading toward," he said, as if it were a given that they would walk out of the hospital together, walk into the next day and the next week and the next month together.

"Logan—"

He cut her off. "It's just a thought I've been having, a thought that I'm really glad you're going to recover, because I'd like to get to know you better. It's not an offer for a lifetime commitment. Just a… Let's take a little time once this is all worked out, see what we think about each another when we aren't dodging bullets or having our stomachs pumped." His eyes were dark and intense, his expression as soft as a winter sunset. "That's it. Nothing you need to get your bloomers in a bunch about."

That made her laugh, which made her head pound harder, which made her groan. "Bloomers in a bunch?" she managed, and he smiled.

"My grandmother's favorite expression. I can still remember her saying it. I also remember how I felt when you collapsed at the church—as if I might be losing something wonderful before I'd ever had it. I'm not coward enough to turn away from that, Harper. I want to know what it meant, what it means."

"Shelby women have never been good at relationships, Logan. My mother had a new boyfriend every other day. Lydia was the same way until she met Gabe, and even that relationship wasn't what it should have been."

"And you?" he asked, pulling a chair closer to the bed, sitting so that they were knee to knee, eye to eye. She wanted to believe that there was something there, something they could build on, something they could walk through life with.

She wanted it so badly her eyes burned and her chest ached.

"Just one serious boyfriend through high school and most of college. We had our wedding planned, our future planned."

"But?"

"He decided to have a future with someone else." That was all she was going to say, because there was nothing else to add. It was enough to prove her point. She and her sister and mother? They had no idea how to choose a guy who would always choose them, and that was what Harper wanted—someone who would walk into a room filled with women and have eyes only for her, thoughts only for her.

"I'd like to say that I'm sorry," Logan murmured. "But I'm not. You deserved better, and if you'd ended up with him, you would never have gotten that."

"You're right, but that isn't the point of the story."

"What is?"

"That Shelby women and men don't mix. We always end up worse off for the experience."

"Seems to me," he said, "that you're putting a whole lot of stock in the past and not a whole lot of faith in what God can do. He changes things, makes the impossible possible."

"I know."

"You just don't think he'll do it for you?"

"I—"

A nurse bustled into the room, ending the conversation before it had really begun. Harper should have been relieved. She should have been happy. Somehow, though, she felt sad, disappointed, sure that she'd missed an opportunity she wouldn't have again.

She couldn't meet Logan's eyes, didn't want

to see the disappointment she thought would be there.

She was too afraid to admit that she wanted exactly what Logan did because she was terrified of being hurt again.

She frowned as the nurse checked her vitals, talked about the long-term impacts of ethylene glycol poisoning. Apparently there were a lot, but Harper's blood work looked good. She hadn't needed dialysis. A dozen things could have gone wrong but hadn't.

She was lucky. That was what the nurse said.

Harper thought it was something a lot more beautiful—grace, divine intervention. She'd almost eaten the second cookie Maggie offered because she'd been feeling a little light-headed, a little sick. She'd refused because that sickness had come on pretty quickly after the first cookie, and she'd thought maybe she was having a reaction to the frosting or the sugar.

Maggie...

Had she mixed antifreeze into the cookie frosting?

An image of the doctor crouching next to Hannah filled her mind. That had been the face of compassion and of sympathy. Not the face of a killer.

"Where's Sandra?" she asked, something

nudging at the back of her mind, a smidge of a warning that she thought she'd be wise to heed.

Sandra.

Interesting that Harper would think of her. Logan had been thinking about her, too. He'd spent the past three days sitting next to Harper's hospital bed calling himself every kind of fool for not thinking about the threat that could be hidden in Christmas cookies.

Maggie was the simple answer to how antifreeze had gotten in the cookies. She'd taken the cookies from Sandra, scraped off the frosting, added the coolant and refrosted the batch. That was what the police were speculating, because Sandra had baked the cookies at Gabe's house. He'd been in the kitchen with her. He'd helped her frost them and pack them in the plastic container.

His story and Sandra's matched, but there were a couple of hours between the cookies being finished and being handed over to Maggie. Sandra could have added the poison during that time. Or Adeline could have.

Someone was lying, and the police had found antifreeze in the trunk of Maggie's car. Her fingerprints were on the bottle and the lid.

An open-and-shut case.

Except it wasn't.

Maggie was a smart lady. It seemed as if she was too smart to let her crime be so obvious.

Just thinking about it made his muscles tense and his chest tight.

"Sandra is in a hotel. The police escorted her here for questioning after the hospital confirmed that you were poisoned. She didn't want to intrude on Gabe and the Stanleys, so she's kept herself holed up there."

"Adeline?"

"Same, but she returned home after she passed a lie detector test."

"Did Sandra pass?"

"Yes."

"And Maggie failed?" she pressed, ignoring the nurse's suggestion that she lie down.

"She passed, too."

"Then, why is she in jail?"

"Because the antifreeze was found in her car, and she's the one who insisted you eat the cookie."

"She was trying to help." She frowned. "I think. My memory is a little fuzzy."

"It might be for a while," the nurse said as she checked Harper's IV. "Everything looks good. If there's anything you need, just ring for me."

"I need to get out of here."

"That's not going to happen until you can keep solid foods down and—"

"Bring me a burger," Harper said with such grim determination, Logan smiled. "I'll show you how easily I can keep it down."

"Not today. We'll try some clear liquids first. Tomorrow, we'll see if the doctor—"

"I'm not going to be here tomorrow," Harper said firmly. "I want to be discharged tonight."

"The doctor—"

"Can you ask him to come in here so I can discuss it with him?"

"If you insist," the nurse responded. "But I can tell you right now, he won't sign the release forms."

She strode out of the room, rubber-soled shoes tapping on the floor, and Harper dragged blankets up around her shoulders and stood.

"This isn't a good idea," Logan muttered, grabbing her waist and holding her steady.

She smiled, her face pale as paper, her eyes rimmed red. She had black circles beneath her eyes and hollows beneath her cheekbones, but she looked about twenty times better than she had the day she'd collapsed. "I think it's a great idea. I've always hated hospitals," she said. "Are my clothes around?"

"Harper, you're in no shape to leave."

"I'm in no shape to sit around waiting for answers," she responded, but she didn't step away. "Those cookies could have been for me, Logan, but I'm worried that they were for Amelia. If she'd eaten one, she might not have survived."

"I know."

"Who would gain from her death?"

"Maggie is at the top of the list. She might not want a ready-made family," he said, tossing out one of the accusations the FBI had lobbed at the doctor. "She was with Gabe the night your sister was murdered, but there's a possibility she orchestrated the crime, that she hired Norman Meyers to do the dirty work for her, because she wanted your sister out of the way."

"Then, why not kill Amelia, too?"

"Because she was Gabe's child? That's what the FBI is saying. I say it doesn't make a whole lot of sense. Especially this new twist—to suddenly reveal that Amelia is alive and then try to kill her? I can't wrap my mind around that."

"Neither can I, so why is she in jail?"

"Circumstantial evidence? Speculation?" Or the police and the FBI were trying to bring the real killer out of hiding.

That had occurred to Logan, and it had occurred to Chance and Malone.

"What about the woman who claimed to be Amelia's mother?"

"She definitely wasn't Maggie. Both the Stanleys were certain of that."

"Was her name on the birth certificate?"

"That's an interesting question," he responded, nudging her backward until her legs hit the bed.

She sat, brushing her hand over her cotton hospital gown, smoothing wrinkles from the fabric. "Why?"

"Someone broke into the Stanleys' home a few months ago. Took some jewelry and a couple of hundred dollars they had hidden in a vase. They thought that was all that was missing. Until yesterday."

"Let me guess," she said. "The birth certificate is missing."

"Right. They do know the birth mother's name, though. At least, the name that was on the certificate. Jamie S. Daniels. The father's name was listed as Ralph Daniels. The FBI can't find any record of him."

Harper sighed, her shoulders slumping beneath the blanket. "What a mess."

"It is, but it's going to get cleaned up."

"I hope you're right."

"Trouble never lasts forever," he said, dropping onto the bed beside her, wrapping his arm around her shoulders.

He didn't need to urge her to move closer. She moved without prodding, her arm bumping his as she leaned against him. He wanted to tell her everything would be okay. He wanted to promise her that her niece would be okay, that she'd be okay. More than anything, he wanted to be able to look her in the face and tell her that it was over, that the killer was in jail and she was safe.

He couldn't do that, so he stroked her silky hair and said nothing.

"I'm a mess," she murmured, touching a strand of hair that had fallen over her shoulder.

"You're beautiful," he replied, and she shifted so that they were eye to eye.

"You shouldn't say things like that, Logan."

"Why not?"

"Because I might start believing that you mean them."

"I do," he said simply, and she smiled the same sad-eyed smile he'd seen a dozen times before.

"For now."

"How about we let that be enough? How about we just enjoy that God has given it to us, and we see where it leads?"

She studied his face, her hand resting on his arm, her expression unreadable. Finally, she nodded. "I think that's a great idea, Logan. I really do."

His cell phone buzzed, and she scooted back, her hand falling away.

He glanced at his phone anyway and frowned when he saw Chance's number.

He answered quickly, knowing his boss wouldn't be calling if there wasn't trouble. "What's up?"

"Amelia is missing." The words were blunt and to the point, the urgency behind them masked by the brevity of the sentence.

"How?"

"She disappeared during recess. Another kid saw her talking to a woman, but that's the last time she was seen."

"Any description of the lady in question?"

"Short. Black hair."

It could have been anyone. Could have been, but Logan didn't think it was. He thought it was the missing piece to the puzzle, the one that would snap into place and reveal the full picture. "You know who that sounds like?"

"Sandra. Trust me, the police are well aware of it. Seeing as how she's not at the hotel—"

"I thought the local PD was keeping an eye on her."

"Who?" Harper demanded. He tugged her close, shifted the phone so she could hear.

"She slipped out at some point. They knocked on her door when they got the call about Amelia. She didn't answer. Looks as if she might have picked the lock on a door that connected her room to the one next to it."

"Looks as if they weren't keeping a very careful eye on her," he muttered.

"At this point, it doesn't matter. Amelia is gone, and we're going to find her. Get Malone and meet me at the church."

"Harper—" He met her eyes.

She shook her head, mouthed, "I'll be fine."

He wasn't worried about her being fine. He was worried about her staying put and staying safe.

"I've already asked the local PD to send someone to the hospital. If Sandra is the killer, there's no telling what she'll do." He disconnected, and Logan stood, dragging Harper along with him.

"You heard what he said?" he asked.

She nodded, her eyes wide with fear. "Amelia is missing. The police think Sandra might have her."

"Not that part," he said, grabbing his coat from the back of the chair and shrugging into it. "The part about the police coming here."

"I heard that, too."

"Good. All you have to do is stay put. Don't go anywhere. Don't talk to anyone. Just stay here until I come back for you."

"Logan—" she started, but he didn't have

time for an argument, didn't have time to list all the reasons she needed to do what he said.

"I can't concentrate on finding your niece if I'm worried about your safety. Promise me you'll stay here."

She hesitated, then nodded. "I promise."

That was all he needed.

He dropped a quick kiss on her forehead and ran out the door, his mind racing. Sandra missing. Amelia gone. The young girl had just been found. He couldn't imagine her being lost again, maybe lost for good.

For her parents' sake, for Gabe's and for Harper's, mostly, though, for Amelia's, Logan couldn't let that happen.

FOURTEEN

She planned to do exactly what she'd promised.

Eight hours later, she was still planning that.

She'd gotten the doctor to have her IV removed, insisted on having her clothes returned. She'd changed back into jeans and the oversize sweater she'd gotten from the safe house. She'd eaten a bowl of clear Jell-O, sipped hot broth, paced the hospital room, the memory of Logan's hasty kiss the only thing keeping her from opening the door and finding a ride to the church.

She'd promised that she'd stay where she was.

And she wasn't going to break that promise.

She wanted to, though.

She did.

Outside, the sun had set, flakes of snow drifting lazily from the dark sky. Christmas carols played, the strains of a familiar hymn drifting through the closed door, and she paced more.

There was nothing else she could do.

She'd tried to call Gabe. He hadn't answered.

She'd questioned the police officer stationed outside her door, and he'd been able to tell her only that they were working closely with the FBI.

Cold comfort when Amelia was missing.

Lost. Found. Lost again. Because of Sandra? Could she have done this to Lydia? To Amelia?

If so, why?

She dragged her cell phone from her pocket, dialed Gabe again. Still no answer. She tucked it back into her pocket, and the lights went out.

Just like that the room went black.

She stumbled to the door, yanked it open.

An emergency generator roared to life, and dim lights illuminated the hallway.

"Stay in your room until I figure out what's going on," the police officer ordered, nudging her back inside and closing the door.

She waited, breathless, as people ran past the room. An emergency announcement blared, demanding that everyone shelter in place.

No way. If there was trouble, she'd rather face it head-on than cower in a room waiting for it to find her.

She opened the door again, came face-to-face with a woman she had no expectation of seeing.

Sandra, her eyes alight with some strange energy, her mouth twisted in a macabre smile.

"Harper. Finally. I've been waiting to reunite you with your niece. I've got a wonderful little party planned."

"What are you—"

She didn't get the words out.

Sandra pulled a gun from her pocket and jabbed it into Harper's chest. "No questions. We've got no time for them. Amelia is waiting."

"Where—?"

Sandra lifted the gun and slammed it into Harper's cheek with so much force, she saw stars.

"I said no questions. Next time, you'll get worse than that." She grabbed her arm and dragged her through the empty hallway into a stairwell.

She thought they'd head down, but Sandra forced her up. One flight. Then another.

"It was so hard to find a safe place for us to meet. So hard," she said as she opened the stairwell door and shoved Harper out into an empty corridor. No hospital rooms here. No nurses. It looked like offices, and none of them seemed occupied. "Fortunately, I'm persistent, and Amelia is such a sweet girl. A lot more like you than like Lydia."

"You killed Lydia." The comment just slipped out, and Sandra shrugged.

"She was in the way."

"The way of what?"

"My relationship with Gabe. We were lovers, you know. Just one slip before marriage. That's what he called it. He was drunk, but I was sober. I knew what I was doing, because I knew exactly what I wanted. Only the next day, he told me it was a mistake. He told me to forget it and move on. Hard to do when you're carrying the product of it."

"You were pregnant?"

"My daughter was born in New York. She died in New York. Lydia's fault."

"Lydia knew?"

"Of course not," Sandra snapped. "I didn't tell anyone. I thought I'd do the right thing. Have the baby, raise it. Let Lydia and Gabe's relationship die a natural death, then step in and tell him he had a child, show him why we should be together." She shoved Harper around a corner, the gun still in her hand. Harper thought she could have taken it from her, but she had no idea where they were headed, no idea where Amelia was, no idea if she was even still alive.

Please let her be alive, she was praying silently, when something at the far end of the corridor caught her eye. A subtle shifting in the shadows, a flicker of movement in the dim emergency lights.

Logan?

Her heart jumped at the thought, hope soaring as she imagined a dozen armed men moving through the darkness. HEART members were experts at this. The FBI knew what it was doing. The Pennsylvania state troopers were trained for this kind of trouble.

If they were at the end of the corridor, there was a chance Harper and Amelia would survive.

There was a chance anyway.

There was no way Harper was going down without a fight.

She slowed her steps, trying to give help a little more time to arrive.

"If you were going to let the relationship die a natural death," she asked, desperate to keep Sandra talking, to keep her distracted, "why did you kill my sister?"

"I got tired of waiting. Plus, I was tired of hearing her complain about Gabe. She had everything, and she didn't appreciate it. A husband who adored her. A little girl who was alive and healthy. My daughter was dead, because the stress of hiding my pregnancy from the man I loved because your sister had stolen him from me caused preeclampsia. The doctors delivered my little angel at twenty-four weeks. She died three days later. I was alone, and your sister? She just wouldn't shut up about how she wished she was as free as I was. I freed her."

"I think she would rather you'd left her alone."

"Then, she should have shut up! I warned her. I told her that if she didn't start counting her blessings, they might all be taken away. When she didn't listen, I called her up and asked her to meet me. Told her I was only in town for the night. She came with Amelia. I was just going to talk to her, tell her how selfish she was being, but then I realized I could have what I wanted if she weren't around. I could have my daughter. My lover."

"Amelia wasn't your daughter."

"I was going to make her mine, but I couldn't think of a way to explain that to Gabe," she snarled, her eyes wild. "I couldn't think of a way to tell him that I'd done him a favor."

"So you ran with Amelia?"

"I did, but that wasn't going to work, either, was it? I didn't have a living daughter. Mine was dead. My family had never even known about the pregnancy. Neither had my friends. It isn't as if I could have suddenly announced that I had a kid, so I gave her away, went back to New York, packed my stuff and returned to DC to claim what should have been mine all along. Only Gabe didn't give me a second look. He gave me a job, though. I had plenty of qualifications, and we both just acted as if our *little fling* had never happened. Maggie's fault this time." She spat the name. "And there was nothing I could do to make him look away from her. When they got engaged, I knew I had to act."

"By sending me newspaper clippings about Norman Meyer's death, by sending pieces of Amelia's baby blanket?"

"Just a little game, Harper. To draw you out of your hiding place. I figured you couldn't resist anything that had to do with your sister and niece."

"But…why now?"

"Because Maggie was in my way, and I knew you would be, too," she nearly shouted, then took a deep, steadying breath. "I figured if you were dead, there'd be one less person who'd ask questions when I brought Amelia out of hiding. That's what I planned, you know—that Gabe and I would get married, and that one day I'd hire a private detective who would just happen to find the missing child. With you gone, there'd be one less person who would wonder why Maggie hadn't killed her when she killed Lydia. Of course, then I realized that I couldn't have it all. I couldn't have Gabe and my daughter. I had to kill Amelia to make sure Maggie went to jail. Only you stupidly ate the cookies."

"You're crazy."

"Does crazy earn enough money to hire men to do her work for her and convince them that if they don't keep quiet they'll die? Does crazy plan something like this and get away with it?" She cackled with glee. "No, Harper. It doesn't. I'm not crazy. I'm in love."

Sandra opened a door and shoved her into a dark room.

"Only Gabe refused to see that we're meant to be together. He needs to be punished for that."

Somewhere in the darkness a child sobbed, and Harper's pulse leaped.

"It's okay, Amelia," she called into the darkness. "Everything is going to be fine."

"It *is* going to be fine," Sandra mocked. "Right as rain, Amelia. Once I have what I want."

"What do you want?" Harper asked, backing away from Sandra's shadowy form, moving toward the sound of the crying child.

"For Gabe to suffer the way I have. For him to want something that he'll never get. For him to spend the rest of his life with a hole in his heart."

Harper's stomach churned, her heart thudding with terror.

Behind her, something moved. She turned and nearly stumbled over her niece.

"Amelia?" She knelt, her eyes adjusting to the darkness, her mind racing with a thousand things she could do, should do. But which ones would save them?

Amelia was bound, hands behind her back, ankles together. Tall for her age. Still blond. Her eyes shaped just like Lydia's, her face a pale oval in the darkness.

"It's going to be okay," she told the crying girl, and she prayed that it was true.

"She's going to kill us," Amelia responded through her tears, and Harper knew she was right. Sandra had one purpose, one goal. She didn't care if she survived it, didn't care if she lived or died. She wanted Gabe to suffer.

There was a chair nearby. A table. Nothing light enough to lift with ease, but Harper was strong from years of hauling clay, and she thought she just might be able to use the chair as a weapon.

"She's not going to kill us," she assured Amelia, frantically tugging at the ropes that bound the girl's wrists while Sandra locked the door.

Sandra laughed. "You're a good aunt, trying to make her feel better. And honestly, I'm tempted to let her live. She's only a year younger than my Autumn would have been. She almost is my Autumn, since I gave the pastor and his sweet, sweet wife Autumn's birth certificate."

"I'm sorry you lost your daughter," Harper

said, sure she heard something moving outside the door.

If Sandra heard, she didn't let on.

She was pacing back and forth in front of the door, head down as she muttered. "Not as sorry as Gabe is going to be when he loses everything,"

Harper leaned down, whispered in Amelia's ear, "I'm going to distract her. You hop to the door, unlock it and scream as if every monster in the world is chasing you."

"They are," Amelia said, but she levered up onto her knees and scooted along the floor. No more sobs. No more tears. Harper didn't know if she understood what was happening. She had no idea if Amelia even knew who she was. They were in this together, though, and the eight-year-old seemed willing to try anything to escape.

"What are you doing?" Sandra screeched, turning from the door. "I told you not to move."

She raised the gun, and Harper knew this was it, her one chance. Her last chance.

She grabbed the chair and swung it so hard, her shoulders popped. It slammed into Sandra with enough energy to send her flying.

The gun went off, the world rocking with the force of the explosion.

Someone screamed. Screamed again.

And Sandra was up, lunging toward Harper, the gun pointed, Amelia's screams filling the air.

Was she hurt? Unlocking the door? Going for help?

Harper grabbed Sandra's gun arm and shoved it to the side as she fired again. The bullet whizzed past, slamming into the wall.

"You are going to pay!" Sandra screamed, throwing her weight against Harper, forcing her into the wall.

It knocked the breath out of her, but Amelia was still screaming, the sound echoing through the room, filling Harper with adrenaline and more terror than she'd ever felt. She had to save her niece. Had to.

She punched Sandra's stomach, shoving her back, knocking her off her feet. The gun fell to the floor and skidded under the desk.

"Hurry, Amelia!" she shouted as she dived after the gun, because her niece was still at the door, struggling with the lock.

"I can't!" the girl cried. "It's stuck."

"You have to," she responded, her hand on the barrel of the gun, the cool metal beneath her fingers.

But Sandra was there, slamming her fist down on Harper's.

"You will not win," she growled, snagging the gun.

Harper rolled away, putting the desk between them to make sure Sandra was facing away from the door.

It was all she could do. The only thing she could offer.

Please, God. Please save Amelia.

The door finally opened, muted light from the hallway spilling in. People spilling in. Shadows rushing forward, people shouting, and Sandra was on her feet again, the gun still in her hand. She raised it and pointed it straight at Harper's heart.

"Die!" she yelled, and the world exploded again.

One shot. That was all Logan had. All he needed.

One shot, and the gun flew out of Sandra's hand, clattering to the floor as the lights suddenly went on.

Blood. It dripped onto the ground, pooling at Sandra's feet.

She was still standing, though, the arm Logan had shot hanging limply by her side.

"All I wanted," she said as an FBI agent rushed in and pulled her good arm up behind her back, "was what I deserved."

Then the agent was leading her away, and Logan was looking into Harper's face.

"Thank the Lord," he whispered, and she walked forward into his arms as if she'd always been there, would always be there.

"I thought Amelia was never going to get the door open," she said, her hands on his waist, her head pressed against his chest.

"I thought we were never going to get inside. An agent had run for the key, but I heard the gunshot..." And his heart had nearly stopped.

"Sandra is certifiably crazy."

"Would have been a good thing to know before now," he said, his voice gruffer than he'd intended.

He should never have left the hospital. If he'd lost Harper, he would never have forgiven himself for doing it.

"She covered it well." Harper shuddered, pulling back a little. "Where's Amelia?"

"Here," Malone said, his arm around the little girl's shoulder as he led her back across the room.

"I'm sorry, Aunt Harper," Amelia said, her eyes filled with fear. "I was so scared my fingers wouldn't work."

"You did great, honey." Harper knelt so that they were eye to eye. "You're very brave. Just like your mother was."

"You mean Lydia? I remember her," Amelia said. "Just a little. And Gabe, and—" she glanced over her shoulder, her eyes wide with fear "—the monster, but I just thought it was all a dream, you know? I never thought any of it was real."

"I'm sorry, honey." Harper reached out, and Amelia hugged her. They stayed that way as the police moved in and an emergency team rushed to make sure they weren't injured. Stayed there, in each other's arms. Reunited at last. Safe at last.

This was why Logan did what he did.

This was what he'd devoted his life to.

This made all the late nights, the high risk, the long weeks away from home worth it.

Harper met his eyes and smiled, a dark bruise on her cheek painful and swollen, but the look on her face one of joy, contentment, love.

"Thank you," she said quietly, and he crouched beside her, tucking a piece of silky hair behind her ear.

"I don't want your thanks, Harper," he said honestly. What he wanted was forever, for always, for every moment they could have together.

He didn't say that to her.

He didn't want to scare her away.

She didn't look scared, though. She looked as if maybe she wanted the same thing he did. To walk forward together and see where the road would lead them.

She took his hand, kissed his palm, closed his fist around the spot.

"What's that for?" he asked, smiling for the first time since he'd realized that Sandra had taken Amelia and headed to the hospital.

"A piece of my heart."

"That," he murmured, "is the best gift I have ever received."

And then he leaned in and kissed her gently as Amelia giggled in her arms.

FIFTEEN

Christmas.

Not a day for nerves.

A day for hope, for renewal, for promises and for joy.

But Harper *was* nervous. She eyed herself in the mirror and wondered if she should have worn the black dress instead of the blue one. Both were new. Both had been purchased before she'd made the trip to North Carolina.

Before *they'd* made the trip.

Logan had invited her entire family—a family that had grown threefold in the past month. Not just her and Picasso anymore. Gabe and Maggie. Camden, Hannah and Amelia. Even Adeline had come, because she was part of the new family that had been built, and no one wanted to leave her behind.

"You look beautiful, Aunt Harper," Amelia said quietly from the doorway of the room.

"So do you, sweetie," Harper said, motioning for her to enter. "I love your dress."

"Mom made it for me." She lifted the hem of a pretty red dress and turned so that the fabric swirled around her. "Maggie and Gabe bought me another one, but I like this better. So I told them I'd wear that to school the first day after break."

"I think that's a wonderful idea," Harper said, giving her niece a gentle hug.

Despite all the trauma she'd been through, Amelia seemed to be adjusting well. Probably because Maggie and Gabe had been married by a justice of the peace and relocated to Pennsylvania. Neither wanted to tear Amelia out of the arms of the couple who had loved her for four years. They'd moved into a house down the street from Camden and Hannah, and they were working on building a family that included both sets of parents.

It was tough, but for the sake of Amelia, all the adults were trying, and they all seemed happy.

Watching Gabe and Maggie make decisions together had shown Harper what love could be if both people were willing to compromise, to sacrifice, to listen and learn. Camden and Hannah seemed to be just as connected to each other.

It gave her hope that maybe that kind of love

was just around the corner, that maybe what she felt when she was with Logan would last.

Logan…

Just thinking about him made her pulse jump and her cheeks warm.

Coming to North Carolina with him was part of a fragile new beginning that they both wanted.

She'd told him that she'd given him a piece of her heart. The truth was, he had much more of her heart than that. He had every part of it. One day, she'd tell him that. Maybe today. Their first Christmas together.

"You look scared," Amelia said, cocking her head to the side, the gesture so like one of Lydia's that Harper's heart ached.

"You look like Lydia," she said, because both sets of parents had agreed that talking about what had happened was the key to healing.

"And like you," Amelia responded. "I'm glad. You're very pretty, and you love art. Just like me."

"I didn't realize you were an artist."

"Not yet," Amelia said solemnly. "But one day I will be. I have something for you. My very first pot. Gabe bought me a potter's wheel a couple of weeks ago, and I threw a bowl. I had to try like a million times before I got it right."

"A potter's wheel, huh? That's a nice gift," she

said as Amelia tugged her out of the room and down the wide hallway of the farmhouse that Logan had grown up in. It looked like him— steady and sturdy and strong.

"He's trying to buy my affection. That's what my friends at school say."

"Do you believe that?" Harper asked, biting back a harsh response. Gabe had a lot of faults, but he was doing everything he could to give Amelia a wonderful, stable environment to grow up in.

"At first," Amelia said matter-of-factly, "I did. Then I told Mom that I thought buying someone's affection was stupid, and that I kind of thought Gabe was stupid for trying to do it. She set me to right."

The words coming out of Amelia's mouth made Harper smile. "That sounds just like something your mother would say."

"It is. She likes Gabe and Maggie. She says they're good people, and they want what's best for me. She also says that Gabe isn't buying my affection. He's making up for lost time."

"I think that's true," Harper said, stepping into a room decorated in yellows and blues. Amelia's things were spread out on the bed, her clothes tossed on the floor.

"I guess I think it's true, too," Amelia said, digging into her suitcase. "Dad says that God has a plan for everything and a time for everything, and I think that's right. I think Mom and Dad really needed me, and all the bad things that happened put me right in their arms. And, you know," she said, pulling something out of the suitcase, "I needed them, too. They've taught me a lot of stuff that I don't think Gabe could have, and now we're all together, and that's cool. Not everyone has two sets of parents."

"You're a smart girl, Amelia."

"Maybe," Amelia responded, pulling tissue paper off the thing she was holding to reveal a small clay bowl, the shape just a little lopsided, the colors like a winter storm—grays and whites with hints of blue.

She handed it to Harper.

"I made it for you."

Harper felt the smooth finish, studied the swirling colors. She turned it over, saw that the bottom was painted crisp white, a small red heart in the center.

"This is beautiful," Harper said, and she meant every word of it.

"Mom says I have talent. I don't care about that. I just care about making things that are like what's in my head. This is about us."

"You and your family?"

"Me and you. We're like those colors—kind of whipping around sometimes, wondering where we fit. If we just stop and think about it, though, we realize the truth." She took the bowl, turned it so the heart was showing. "Where we fit is in the hearts of the people who love us."

"That is one of the most beautiful things I've ever heard," Harper said, her eyes burning with tears she didn't want to shed. Not in front of her niece.

"Then, I guess you haven't heard a whole lot of beautiful things," Amelia said with a grin. "Anyway, I was going to wrap it and put it under the tree, but you looked nervous, and I wanted you to know things are going to be okay." She handed the bowl back. "I better go downstairs. Adeline is making pancakes, and all those loud kids will eat them before I get any if I don't hurry."

Amelia flounced out of the room and left Harper standing with the bowl in her hand and tears in her eyes.

She sniffed them away, stepped into the hall and ended up in Logan's arms.

Exactly the place she most wanted to be.

She looked up into his familiar face, his gorgeous dark blue eyes.

He was everything she hadn't thought she needed, everything she'd given up wanting. Everything she'd once prayed that she would have. When she looked at him, Daniel didn't exist; her mother's and sister's terrible track records with men didn't exist. When she looked at him all that existed was the two of them and what they could be together if they were willing to try.

"Wow!" he said. "You look amazing."

"Thank you," she responded, her heart doing a giant flip as she met his eyes. "So do you."

"I couldn't let my brothers dress better than me," he responded, tugging at the hem of his black suit jacket. It fit him like a glove, the sky blue dress shirt he'd paired it with perfect.

"It doesn't matter what any of your brothers wear, you'll still be the wardrobe winner to me," she said, and he smiled.

"You always make me feel as if I can conquer the world, Harper. You know that?"

"It's just clothes," she said with a smile, smoothing his lapel. "Of course, you probably could conquer the world. With HEART backing you, I don't think there's anything you can't do."

"Including getting married and raising a family," he murmured, offering a gentle kiss. "I've been thinking about that a lot."

"About getting married and raising a family?" Her pulse jumped at the thought, hope and exhilaration coursing through her blood. She could imagine having children, making Christmas traditions that would be passed on for generations, reading books to tiny kids and listening to their laughter while they played. She could also imagine being Logan's wife, standing beside him through the good and bad and everything in between.

She could imagine so much more than she'd ever thought would be possible.

All because of Logan.

"I never wanted either of those things until I met you, Harper. Too much responsibility. Too many obligations. With you, though? Those things are like the BB gun I wanted for Christmas when I was ten—something I long for, something I never stop thinking about."

It was her turn to laugh. "You were in Nepal rescuing a missionary team last week, so something tells me marriage and a family weren't the only things you were thinking about."

"Even when I was in Nepal, you were always on my mind, and you're the only reason I want either of those things," he responded, tucking a strand of hair behind her ears and frowning. "You've been crying."

"Not really."

He raised an eyebrow.

"Okay," she admitted. "A little."

"Thinking about your sister?" he asked gently.

"Thinking about how wonderfully things turned out. Despite all the hard times and the challenges and the sorrow. Amelia is in a really good place, and that makes me happy."

"How about you, Harper? Are you in a really good place?" he asked, his hands sliding up her waist, smoothing over her arms, settling on her shoulders. Her breath caught, and she knew what she had to say, what she had to tell him.

All the nerves flew away as she looked into his eyes and all the fear and anxiety disappeared.

"Do you remember when I gave you a piece of my heart?" she asked, and he smiled.

"How could I forget? I carried it with me to Nepal and thought about it every time I got lonely."

That made her smile. He made her smile.

"The thing is," she said, holding up the bowl Amelia had made, "I've been drifting for a long time, trying to figure out where I belong. For a while, I thought I belonged in my cabin, making my pottery and avoiding the world, but I was wrong."

"Were you?" he said, his fingers threading through her hair, his eyes dark and filled with everything she had longed for.

"Yes."

"Have you discovered where you do belong?" he asked, his lips brushing hers, the sweetness of that one touch settling deep into her soul.

"Anywhere you are," she responded. "I love you, Logan. Not with a piece of my heart. With all of it."

"I love you, too," he said. "For now and always."

He kissed her again, sealing their love, sealing a promise of a future together, and then he took her hand and led her down the stairs into the loud and wonderful embrace of their families.

* * * * *

Dear Reader,

There are times when life is hard. We struggle, we worry, we fight to hold on to what we've striven so hard for, but the more we struggle, the harder it is to grasp. It is easy to stand in those moments, wondering where God is. It is easy to think that He has turned from us. Yet the Bible is clear—in the deepest darkness, He is there. In the hardest moments, He is there. He will never leave or forsake those who love Him, and in this promise, we can rest. Whatever your today, I pray that your tomorrow will be bright and filled with His presence.

I love to hear from readers. You can reach me at shirlee@shirleemccoy.com or visit me on Facebook or Twitter.

Blessings,

Shirlee McCoy

LARGER-PRINT BOOKS!

GET 2 FREE LARGER-PRINT NOVELS PLUS 2 FREE MYSTERY GIFTS

Love Inspired®

Larger-print novels are now available...

REQUEST YOUR FREE BOOKS!
2 FREE WHOLESOME ROMANCE NOVELS IN LARGER PRINT
PLUS 2 FREE MYSTERY GIFTS

YES! Please send me **The Montana Mavericks Collection** in Larger Print. This collection begins with 3 FREE books and 2 FREE gifts (gifts valued at approx. $20.00 retail) in the first shipment, along with the other first 4 books from the collection! If I do not cancel, I will receive 8 monthly shipments until I have the entire 51-book Montana Mavericks collection. I will receive 2 or 3 FREE books in each shipment and I will pay just $4.99 US/ $5.89 CDN for each of the other four books in each shipment, plus $2.99 for shipping and handling per shipment.*If I decide to keep the entire collection, I'll have paid for only 32 books, because 19 books are FREE! I understand that accepting the 3 free books and gifts places me under no obligation to buy anything. I can always return a shipment and cancel at any time. My free books and gifts are mine to keep no matter what I decide.

263 HCN 2404   463 HCN 2404

Name	(PLEASE PRINT)	
Address		Apt. #
City	State/Prov.	Zip/Postal Code

Signature (if under 18, a parent or guardian must sign)

Mail to the **Reader Service:**
IN U.S.A.: P.O. Box 1867, Buffalo, NY 14240-1867
IN CANADA: P.O. Box 609, Fort Erie, Ontario L2A 5X3

MMLPBPA15